Finding Hope

By Tarin Breuner

To the VIP children I've met and the many others out there. Keep playing!

1

"Nadia, over here!"

I looked up to see my teammate and best friend, Liv, waving her arms from across the field. I tapped the ball to the left side of the defender, using the outside of my foot, and crossed it directly to Liv's feet as she ran diagonally towards the goal box. After receiving the ball, she only had to dribble a couple of feet before pulling her leg back and kicking it hard into the top corner of the goal.

"Yes!" I cheered as Liv and I ran into each other's arms.

"That shot was beautiful!" I said, still in awe.

"Oh please, I wouldn't have even had a shot if it weren't for your amazing pass, you placed it perfectly!"

"Very good girls," Coach Terry said while walking towards us, "That was a great play, you two are golden together. I'll definitely keep that in mind when drawing our lineup for this weekend." I watched as she made a note on her clipboard. Liv and I smirked at one another gleefully. Coach Terry pulled out her whistle and blew hard to signal the end of practice, "Alright everyone, grab your things and I'll see you on Thursday," she said.

After collecting the balls and equipment we all ran over to the bench to grab our waters. Liv squeezed my arm, jumping up and down excitedly, her blonde ponytail bobbing along with her.

"Did you hear that? She said we were golden, and then mentioned this weekend, she's totally gonna put us as forwards together!"

Soccer had been a bond for me and Liv for as long as I can remember. It's such a huge part of my life and being able to share it with my best friend made it all the better.

"I know!" I smiled back, "This is going to be the best season yet!" I took her arm and we walked off together towards the bike racks. I crouched down to start unlocking my bike; painted in silver with a marron zig-zag over the wheel.

"So, after today we definitely are on the Coach's good side, but that doesn't mean we can slack off. We'll have to be super focused throughout the whole season. Top priority, no distractions," Liv said, throwing her leg over her bike.

"I completely agree," I responded, placing my foot on the pedal and securing the strap of my helmet.

"Ready?" Liv asked.

"Yep," I said as we started to bike away. It was a short ride to Liv's house and we were there in minutes. "I'll see you in class tomorrow," I called as she walked her bike up the driveway. She turned and waved,

"Bye Nadia!" she said before heading inside.

I continued on along a quiet bike path as it wove through an elementary school, a dog park and then on through a neighborhood. As soon as the street turned back into a greenbelt, I had reached my house. We were right on the corner with a small park just to the left of our front door. I rode my bike up to the side of the house, before opening the side gate, and leaving it in the backyard. From there, I went in through the garage and entered the kitchen to find my mom, Inna, stirring a pot over the stove.

"Hi mom," I said, sniffing the air and catching the strong scent of tomato and garlic, "How long until we eat?"

"Wow, you barely made it through the door before asking that, someone must be hungry," she laughed.

"No, actually, I just, if we have some time, I'd like to go practice a little outside, until dinner," I said, tightening my ponytail.

"You just came from practice!" my mom said.

"I know," I said, "But I just moved up an age group so it's more competitive and really important that I play my very best."

"Well honey, I don't think you really need that much extra practice, after all, you've been a top player on every team since you started. But I am glad that you're so dedicated. We probably won't be eating for close to an hour anyway," she considered, "Go ahead, but don't work yourself too hard, you have practice almost every day this week!"

"I know, don't worry, I'm fine. See you in a bit, thanks!" I ran to the backyard to grab my favorite ball and headed back out the gate to the green belt.

I didn't waste any time before practicing kicks, sprints and exhausting serpentine patterns. In my last set I even added a trick component and did the rainbow, where you flick the ball over your head and catch it at your feet on the other side, before shooting the ball between the two trees I was using as makeshift goal posts.

Before long, I heard my mom calling my name from out the back door. I retrieved my ball and ran inside to eat.

2

The next morning, I barely
made it to school before the first bell.
I was so tired from all the soccer
yesterday that I slept past my alarm.
Thankfully, I had my first class with
Liv, and she had enough energy for
the both of us.

"Nadia guess what?" she cried.

"What?" I asked, my chocolate
eyes wide, feeding off her
excitement.

"I ran into some of the other
soccer girls this morning, and Jenna
said that she overheard Coach Terry
on the phone last night when they
were walking towards the parking lot.
And you know what Terry was
saying?! She's applying our team to

the Maydel Tournament! Do you know how huge that would be? That's one of the biggest tournaments in our state! I can't believe it, I mean I know it's this whole application process and nothing's for sure yet but how amazing would that be?!"

"Oh my gosh Liv! That would be incredible! Now we really can't slack off," I said, opening my binder as the clock inched towards the hour.

"Tell me about it," Liv said. "We don't have practice today, wanna meet in the park after school and run some drills ourselves?"

"Yeah, let's do it," I said.

Our teacher moved to the front of the room and Liv quickly turned to face the board.

"Alright class," our teacher began, "We're going to start off today talking about Mesopotamia . . ."

*　　*　　*

Liv and I trained in the park for a few hours before I finally went home. When I got there, my mom didn't look too thrilled.

"Where on earth have you been?" she asked. I gritted my teeth, realizing I had forgotten to borrow a phone to call and tell her what I was doing.

"I was practicing in the park with Liv. I'm sorry, I forgot to tell you, she told me we might be doing that big Maydel tournament and I was just so excited and felt like I needed to practice right away."

"Honey, I get that you were excited but you had all day to let me know and it's not okay that you didn't, I was worried sick!"

"I know mom, I'm sorry, it was my fault completely, I promise it won't happen again."

"It better not or your practice privileges will be revoked," she said sternly.

"Okay," I said.

"Good," she replied. "Now come on, I have to go to the grocery store and you are coming to help carry bags."

"Can I at least shower first?" I asked, sweat still on my face and grass stains all over my shorts.

"Nope, that's what you get," my mom said, "We're going now."

"Okay," I said. "I just hope we don't see anyone."

*   *   *

We were about done with the grocery shopping when I almost ran our cart into another person.

"Sorry!" I said quickly before looking up and realizing who it was. It was my old soccer coach from a few years ago.

"Nadia!" he said. "How have you been?"

"Good, I'm good! I'm just starting a new season so I'm really excited," I said.

"Pete, hi!" my mom walked over and gave him a hug, "It's been so long!"

"Inna, good to see you, and yes well Nadia here was just starting to catch me up," he smiled.

"Yeah but what about you? Have you been coaching much?" I asked.

"I have," he nodded, "But for something a little different." When I looked confused, he continued, "See, over the past couple of years, I have become the head of a soccer program for kids with disabilities."

"What does that mean?" I asked.

"Well it means that they have a physical or mental condition that impairs them from playing in the regular soccer season. So, through this program, these kids, kids of all ages, come and either learn soccer for the first time, or better the skills they have learned with us in previous seasons. They practice basic drills and play in games together, just like you would with your team."

"That's so cool!" I exclaimed.

"What a great opportunity that must give them," my mom said.

"Yes it's wonderful, I'm so proud of it and so attached to all the kids, watching them develop their abilities is incredibly rewarding."

"I can imagine," my mom said.

"And it's all volunteer," he continued. "People come out and work as buddies for the different kids and teach them what they know about soccer. As a matter of fact, you should be old enough now, and if I remember correctly, you were always a good team leader. You should come out and try it!"

"Really? I don't know if I'm qualified," I blushed.

"Sure you are, you're patient, a good teammate, and you have a love for the game of soccer, that's all you need. It's for an hour and a half every Sunday, that's it! I think you'd be great at it and would really enjoy it. What do you say?"

"Um," I turned to my mom and she nodded yes. "Okay, yeah, I'll try it!"

3

"So these kids, our age, younger and older, who wouldn't normally get to play soccer are given this great opportunity to learn like anyone else," I explained to Liv in class the following morning.

"That's cool," she said, combing her fingers through her hair.

"So, you want to do it with me?" I asked hopefully.

"I don't know, I mean it sounds like a good program, but I have a lot on my plate right now. Besides, I spend Sundays with my dad and I don't think he'll be happy if I commit to something else that day," she said with a sideways frown. Liv's parents had been divorced for a few years, but neither left our city, so she splits her time between the two houses. "But don't worry about it," Liv continued, "We have so much going on with our own team right now, you won't be short of a soccer fix."

"Yeah, I guess so," I said, reconsidering my conversation with Coach Pete as our teacher began talking.

*　　*　　*

"Nadia, you told Pete that you would do the program, he's counting on you, and I'm counting on you to stay true to your commitments."

"I know, I told him I'd do it, but Liv can't do it with me and I don't want to go alone."

My mom turned to face me, and tucked a strand of hair behind my ear.

"Honey, I am so happy that you and Liv are such great friends and love doing so many things together. But you can't be so dependent on your friends that you let those friendships get in the way of trying new things, especially when that new thing is something you may really love."

"But I don't even know if I'll be good at it. What if I get there and do or say something wrong?"

"Well, you laugh it off, or if you've offended anyone you apologize, simple as that. And then you move forward. I think you could be really good at it and I think you could really enjoy it as well."

"I don't know," I said.

"And you never will. But, don't you think you'll always be curious about it unless you try?"

"I guess, I just —"

"How about this," my mom cut me off. "How about you promise me that you will at least go to the Buddy training and the first practice, that's it. And after that, if you want to quit, I won't stop you." She looked at me, awaiting my response.

"Okay," I gave in, "I promise that I will wait until after the first practice, to decide if I don't want to do it anymore."

"That's my girl," my mom said, opening her arms for a hug. "Now," she said, "Why don't you help me make dinner?"

"Okay," I laughed.

4

"The basic principles of this program are to keep it safe, simple and fun, for all of the players," Pete explained as he motioned to the PowerPoint slide at the front of the room. "We have to make sure that everyone is both physically, and mentally, safe at all times. We can avoid lots of confusion and conflict by keeping everything very simple. And lastly, we must always remember that having fun is the number one priority."

Sitting there, listening to him go on to explain the rules and precautions only made my nerves kick in more. I tapped my foot anxiously, looking out the window at the fresh cut soccer field, wanting desperately to run out and start playing.

"Nadia?" I felt a tap on my shoulder and turned to see Pete looking at me. "Are you alright?" he asked.

"Um, yeah, why?" I questioned.

"Well, I finished the presentation and everyone else got up to walk to the field and yet, you're still sitting here."

I looked around, noticing for the first time that everyone else had cleared out of the room.

"Yeah, I just, you know, was taking a minute, but I'll head over there now," I said, getting up quickly and heading for the door.

"Nadia," Pete started, I paused in my step. "Everything will be fine, there's nothing to worry about, you'll be great at this."

I smiled softly to myself at that, before leaving the room. As soon as my feet hit the grass, I ran straight towards the pile of equipment and started helping some of the other volunteers set up a field. I grabbed the flag posts, along with another volunteer, and together, we walked to put them on either end of the field.

"So, are you excited for your first day?" he said, after pushing his post in the ground.

"How do you know it's my first day?" I asked.

"Cause it's not mine," he laughed.

"Oh right," I bit my lip.

"I'm Tadd," he said, reaching out his hand.

"Nadia," I said.

"Well Nadia," he said, "It's a great program, I'm sure you'll really like it."

"Thanks, I hope so," I said as we made our way back to the group.

"Here," he said, "I'll introduce you to the Coach."

"Thanks," I said, "But I already know Pete."

"I wasn't talking about Pete, he may run the program, but Keller runs the practices," he explained. "She's sixteen, so probably three or four grades ahead of you, and she's been coming since this program started. About a year and a half ago, Pete moved her up from Buddy to Coach."

Tadd walked ahead of me and grabbed the arm of a tall girl with short dark hair and almond-shaped brown eyes.

"Keller, this is Nadia; Nadia, this is Keller," he said, motioning between the two of us.

"Nadia," she said, "That's a pretty name, where's it from?"

"It's Russian; my mom grew up there."

"Very cool," she said, "I've never met a Nadia before."

"And I've never met a Keller," I smiled.

"Fair enough," she laughed. "So, how did you hear about this program?"

"Um Coach Pete, he was my soccer coach a few years back, I ran in to him the other day and he told me to come check it out," I explained.

"So you play?" she asked.

"Yeah I do," I said. "You?"

"Used to," she said. "I have some knee problems that keep me from playing for real anymore but I still join in on some pick-up games here and there. Tadd and I play in this one group that meets up on Thursday nights, you should come play sometime," she offered.

"Yeah, that'd be great," I said; glad to make friends in this program as soon as possible.

Minutes later, I watched as the kids started arriving, some pairing off with familiar buddies and others joining into a large group circle passing the ball around. I was about to join in to the circle when I heard Pete call me over to the check in area where he stood with Keller.

"Hey Nadia, the two of us were talking and I think I know someone who would be great to pair you with, she just started practicing with us a few sessions ago and I think it would be good for her to have someone specific to work with.

"Uh, okay, yeah," I said nervously, not sure I was ready to work with someone by myself.

"Here she comes now," Pete said, motioning to a girl walking over from the bike path.

"I have to go get everyone started, but let me know if you need anything, okay?" Keller said to me, putting her hand on my shoulder.

"Yeah sure, thanks," I said.

"I'll come check on you in a little bit," she said over her shoulder as she walked back towards the group.

The girl was almost to us now; she had curly hair and light blue eyes, a sharp contrast against her dark skin.

She wore a blue and white jersey, black soccer shorts and cleats.

"Nadia," Pete said, "This is Hope, she---" he was about to say more when I jumped in.

"Wait your name is Hope?" I asked excitedly, "My name means Hope! That's so funny," I smiled. Hope didn't say anything but just looked at me with a confused expression on her face.

"Nadia, Hope is Deaf," Pete told me, "She does not have the power to hear."

I watched as he moved his fingers and hands in front of Hope, and she did the same back to him after he'd finished, then, stepping to the side and smiling at me, clearly showing she understood the introduction.

"At home she uses sign language with her family. I've been learning since she started coming here, there's a class at the community center once a week. Anyway, she's been Deaf of hearing since birth, she can make sound, but for the most part chooses not to, and it's not something we'll ever force."

"But I don't know sign language," I said meekly.

"You don't have to, body language and expression go a lot further than you may realize, especially as you two get to know each other," Pete smiled.

"How can we get to know each other if we can't communicate?" I asked.

"Not all communication is verbal, and believe me, we'd all be a lot better of friends if we would just learn to stop talking every now and then," he laughed. "And don't be so negative, Hope's pretty good at reading lips," he winked before walking away.

"Of course," I mumbled, turning to see Hope staring at me. Unsure of what to do, I rolled the nearest soccer ball over and began touching it between my feet. Back and forth, tap, tap, tap, creating a place of comfort for myself.

Hope watched my feet for a few minutes before looking up and studying my face, I kept my eyes down. I spent my time thinking of what to do, or say, only to come up dry, just stalling until Keller announced it was time for everyone to come together.

5

The rest of the day didn't run any smoother. By the end of the session, I was exhausted over nothing and frustrated over everything. The only real communication I had with Hope all afternoon was our introduction by Pete at the beginning, and our good-bye waves at the end. Outside of that, I was sure that Hope had understood nothing else I had tried to do all practice long.

Biking back along the greenbelt, and up to my house, my frustration was only growing. As I went inside, I came to find my mom, studying some papers at the eat-in table by the kitchen.

"Hi honey," she peeked over the rim of her reading glasses,

"How'd it go? I want to hear all about it!"

"It was horrible," I said slowly, taking a seat next to her.

"Why?" she looked completely taken aback.

"Because," I started, "I was assigned to work with Hope, a girl a little younger than me, who's Deaf! We have no way to communicate, she can't hear, she can talk, but chooses not to, and I don't know sign language so I can't talk to her, and I just, I'm terrible at it. Clearly it's just not something I'm meant to do."

"Sounds like you're being pretty judgmental," my mom said.

"I didn't mean to be, I don't have any problem with her at all. I'm sure she's great and I don't see being Deaf as a bad thing, but I don't really know anything about it, so I feel helpless and I don't like feeling that way."

"I didn't mean you were being judgmental of Hope, although you could probably talk about her more respectfully," she looked at me and I bowed my head, "But what I meant, was that you were being judgmental of yourself."

"Huh?"

"You're saying you can't talk to her, and you're terrible at it, and you don't know anything about it," she said.

"All true," I reiterated.

"No," my mom said. "You can talk to her without words, and if you want to talk to her with words she can understand, you have the power to learn her language while she doesn't have the power to learn yours. You say you're terrible at it after your first day, nobody's good their first day on the job, even if it's what their meant to do. You know why? Because the things you're meant to do, aren't the things that you do perfectly the first time, those are just things you can do. The things you're meant to do, are those that make you feel something in your heart, the things that you feel are worth it to work for. But that's not something I can tell you," she smiled sympathetically and ruffled my hair as she stood up to grab her recipe book.

"I'm gonna go do some sprints, clear my head," I said, after taking a few minutes to sit and ponder.

"Don't be too long," my mom said, "It'll be getting dark soon."

I got up and made my way to the back door, where I could take a few steps and slip out the side gate. But as I was beginning to slide open the door, I paused and turned back to face the kitchen.

"Mom?"

"Yes honey?"

"If Hope has the ability to create sound and talk, why do you think she chooses not to?" I wondered; my mom studied me before looking off, as though considering an old memory.

"When I was first moved here from Russia, just a young girl coming in to a new country, and culture, that I knew nothing about, I was still learning English. I think a lot of people, specifically people who learn a new language as more of a hobby, whether it's for school, or work, or themselves, they usually want to speak to, and practice with, native speakers as much as possible. But when you're learning a new language because you have to, not because you want to, it's different. It's much scarier and creates a sense of discomfort. When I came, I felt like everyone was trying to make me an American before I was ready, before I knew the language or even before I knew the way of life. I felt like I was being forced to speak a language that didn't feel like mine, and it was for other people, not myself. It should be for yourself. It became that way later for me, because I chose it to be, but it took time.

I would imagine that Hope feels similarly. That when people are trying to make her talk, she feels forced into the box of what they want her to be, and not what she is. It doesn't feel right to her because what speaking is to a non-Deaf person, it isn't to a Deaf person. The same way that no matter how much I am a part of this country, my language will first and foremost, still be Russian. And no matter how much you learn about your heritage, or how much time you spend there, your first language will always be English, and your first home, will always be America. And that's okay.

We don't need to be the same. We don't need to be the same, or come from the same thing as any of our loved ones. Differences should be embraced, for they make you stronger."

I considered her words as I walked out the yard. I understood what she said, I think, and I believed it too. I knew that I wanted to try again, that I wasn't the type of person to give up on the first try. But I couldn't shake the fact, that for the first time, I was scared to try.

6

"Nadia, it's Friday," my mom said plainly.

"This is true," I said, spreading out my homework sheets across the table, and debating my divide-and-conquer strategy.

"And?" she raised a brow.

"And?" I asked back, unsure of what she was implying, she sighed.

"Have you made your decision about the soccer program yet?" she asked.

"Oh, that . . ."

"Yes that. The next session is in two days, at this point I'm debating saying to you that you have to do it, even if the answer is no, because at this point it would be too rude and last minute, to back out on Pete," she put her hands on her hips.

"I'll have an answer by tonight, I promise," I said at her wavering expression. "But," I added, "Not right now, because I have to go meet Liv in the park," I bee-lined for the back door.

"What about your homework?"

"That's what the weekend is for, be back soon!" I called over my shoulder, heading out the door.

"But you have a game tomorrow!" she reminded me, but I was already gone.

*   *   *

"So I told my mom I would make a final decision tonight," I bit my lip after recounting my whole do-or-not-do debate about Hope and the soccer program. Liv stood in front of me, practicing her juggling skills, bouncing the ball between her knees, up to her head, and back to her knees.

"Liv?"

"Yeah?"

"Well, you're not saying anything, what do you think?" I asked.

"I think you only went to one session and it's already caused you a bunch of stress and distraction, which isn't good. Hope will get another partner. I say quit."

She said it as though it were the most obvious answer in the world, which made me wanna sway in her direction. Maybe it was that simple. Maybe I should just quit. I tried, and it didn't go well, and I only promised one session so I'm really not stepping out early, in a way.

"We both just need to focus on this season of soccer and our team, nobody else's," Liv said.

"Maybe you're right," I said.

"If you say so," Liv said, "Now come on, let's play!"

We continued to kick the ball around for another half hour, not even realizing the time, when I heard my mom calling from the backyard.

"I better go see what's up," I said, starting to jog away, "See you at the game tomorrow!"

"See ya!" Liv waved, shoving the ball in her backpack.

My mom was back inside by the time I reached the house. I walked in and saw that her back was turned.

"What's up?" I asked. "Dinner?"

"Not quite," she said, turning to reveal the phone in her hand, "You're sister," she extended her arm and I snatched the phone with a huge smile.

"Lesya!" I cried, taking the call to my room, "How are you?" I asked, sitting on my bed.

"I'm good, surviving," she said with a tired voice.

"You always are," I said, turning to my bed-stand to touch the picture of her in uniform. "What's it like over there?" I asked, worry in my voice.

"The same," she said, "Only colder," she laughed. It was good to hear her laugh.

"Save any lives today?" I asked.

"I treated a soldier with a leg wound, his name's Jon, and he looks like he'll be doing pretty well in just a little bit here," she said. "But you know, you can't save them all, or at least that's what I keep telling myself," I could hear the heartbreak behind her words.

"Well, I'm proud of you. I always am," I said.

"Thank you Nadia. Now enough on me, tell me about you."

"Well, I'm on a new team this season and it looks like we're going to be really good, we might be going to this huge tournament in a couple months but we don't know for sure yet."

"That's great. Mom tells me that you started doing this volunteer program where you help kids with disabilities. I think she said you were partnered with a girl named Hope? Just like you," I heard her smile.

"Um yeah I was, but I don't think I'm going to do it anymore," I said awkwardly.

"How come?" she asked.

"Well, I wasn't sure, and then I was talking to Liv today and she pointed out the stress it's caused me and the fact it's made me distracted from our team and kind of helped sway me in the right direction I guess."

"Just because it's the direction you've come to, I wouldn't call it the right one," Lesya said. "You know I love Liv but she's full speed ahead with soccer, and having you as a best friend, anything that pulls away from that isn't going to be something she likes, but it's not about her, it's about you. Clearly it matters to you."

"What do you mean?" I asked.

"Well," she said, "If it's been causing you stress then you've been thinking about it and worrying over it, a lot. That tells me that you care about it. If it didn't matter to you at all, then you would just quit without a second thought. But you've been putting it off, probably out of fear."

I bit my lip, sometimes I hated how well she knew me.

"I don't want you to do it to make me happy, or mom happy, or Pete happy, or even Hope happy. We can all find that on our own. What I want you to do, is whatever is going to make you happy. What's your gut telling you?"

"I'm conflicted, I think I just ---"

"Nadia? Wait hold on one second, the alarm's going off. One second . . . Nadia? I'm sorry, they're calling me in, I have to go, I'll try to call again soon, okay? I'm sorry, I love you."

"I love you too," my voice broke, "Stay safe okay?" the phone buzzed off and I let it drop to the floor as a tear rolled down my cheek.

"You're going to keep doing it?" Liv asked with genuine surprise.

"Yeah, I decided that I want to give it another try, a real try, ya know? This is something that could really matter, make a difference in someone's life. My mom and sister both give so much for other people, all the time. I just think I should start doing the same."

"But, you would be giving more to your teammates, people you've already committed to, if you quit."

"It's different. Just trust me on this one, okay?" I pleaded; she nodded but it felt vacant. I watched as she picked up the nearest ball and moved to the side to start dribbling practice.

"I talked to Lesya last night," I said quietly; Liv immediately softened.

"How is she?" she asked.

"Strong as ever," I gave a weak smile.

"And how are you?' Liv asked, putting her arm on my shoulder.

"Okay. It's just hard, ya know? Not having her here, and just knowing all the trauma that she's exposed to, every day," I said. "I just want her to be safe, and be herself again, she hasn't sounded the same since she left," my expression dropped.

"I'm sorry," Liv said, "I know I can never understand what it's like to have her overseas, just like we'll never know what it's like for her to actually be overseas. But we just have to have hope, and you've got a lot of that," she poked me in the arm, and actually got me smiling. "And I'm always here for you okay, always?" she made me look her in the eye and after a minute I started nodding.

"Always."

8

"Alright guys, we're going to start a scrimmage about half way through practice. So, until then, everyone can pair up and work with their assigned partners as they come in," Keller said, squatting on the ground, pumping up balls.

I bent down to double-knot my shoe laces when I felt a shadow looming over me. Tadd dropped next to me and tilted his head to read the name in block letters along my charm bracelet,

"Lesya?" he asked.

"My sister," I responded quickly, not wanting to think about it. He took the hint and stood along with me, running his hand through his hair.

"How are you feeling about working with Hope again today?" he asked.

"Good, I mean, okay I guess? I want to be here and I want it to go well, I just feel like I have no idea what I'm doing, and I don't want to mess up again," I admitted; Tadd laughed.

"Trust me, none of us really know what we're doing. It's not about expertise, it's about connection. Don't think of Hope as an assignment you have to figure out, just think of her as a new friend you want to get to know," he said, I looked up and nodded slowly.

"That's good advice," I said, "Thanks."

"No problem," he said, walking over to help Keller set up the field as kids began arriving.

I watched buddies and kids join together with each new arrival, starting drills, passing, some just talking but all working together with ease. I envied how simply it appeared to go for everyone else, my own anxiousness growing with each car door opening, waiting to see who it would be next. Before too long, I saw Hope make her way up from the parking lot, hesitantly, I walked to meet her, hoping I appeared more confident than I was.

I waved at her and smiled as I got close, she waved back somewhat timidly, but in her eyes, I could tell she wanted to give it another try too. I grabbed the ball closest to us and gestured for her to follow me to the side of the field. She came up next to me as I set the ball on the line. I began rolling it back on my foot and back to the line again, moving a couple inches to the side with each stride. I could feel her watching me intently as I demonstrated back and forth. After about 15 reps, I tapped the ball and moved off of it, pointing for her to do the same. She took it and followed suit, struggling at first but finding her own stride as the reps grew in numbers.

I watched in amazement at the effort she put into her precision with the ball. It became increasingly clear how much she cared about her performance. She didn't look to me for approval, but instead herself. I could feel my respect and understanding growing, seeing we may have more in common than our names.

When she felt she had done a good enough job, she stopped on her own and tapped the ball, then pointing for me to do the same. I laughed, applauding her confidence and accepting the challenge. We went on against each other for another 15 minutes until the first water break.

As all the others went to grab their waters and take a few minutes in the shade, I took a ball to the corner of the field and began practicing my favorite move: the rainbow. I took the ball between my feet from the back, and flipped it over the back on my head, to land directly back at my feet ahead of me;

then going into a direct dribble sprint down the field as though in a real game. I continued practicing it over and over, hoping one day to have the confidence to use it in a real game, but my coach always discouraged it, said it was too risky.

I don't know how long Hope had been watching before I noticed her standing by the tree nearest me. She seemed fascinated by the move, watching everything I did, every muscle movement, as though trying to memorize.

I waved her over and did it again, slower this time, for her to see up close. After a couple times like that, and another few all the way through, I handed it off to her, and watched as she began finding her ground with the move. It was one of the hardest to learn, and more unique than anything you would do at a regular practice. I had taken it upon myself to learn independently, having seen it done by a player on my favorite Russian team.

Hope grew frustrated at her inability to immediately mimic me, the way she had with my earlier drill. I wasn't sure how to communicate with her that it takes time, and I myself didn't learn it even close to instantly. As I thought about how to express that to her, Hope watched me as though she knew there was something I wanted to say. I started by putting my hand over my heart to get her attention, and make it clear I was referring to myself. From there, I did the rainbow again in front of her, and followed it by slowly rolling my hands over each other and offering a frustrated expression as I pointed to my fake watch, hoping to emphasize how many times I had to practice before I learned. She seemed to understand as she giggled and nodded, then giving it another try with less intention for perfection.

Time seemed to be disappearing quickly, as it felt like only minutes later, Keller announced it was time to start the team scrimmage. The kids were given pennies, split in half to play two sides, Hope was on red team; as we buddies stood on the side lines, cheering and occasionally cycling in as aids to the game.

I watched with pride as I noticed Hope taking the time to practice ball control as we had before. Amazement showered over me from the difference between this session and the last, and I smiled as I watched the kids play around with joy all over their faces; knowing in that moment, I had made the right decision to come back.

"On your right!" Liv called, waving her hand as I scanned the field.

I placed the ball softly, and right at her feet. She took it up the field with ease. A defender jumped in front of her and she tapped the ball to the side, just barely out of their reach. I ran with her; she came upon the sweeper, and almost lost the ball, but they hesitated and tripped, giving her the opportunity to touch the ball backwards, and then around, the same way I had taught Hope, before jumping over their leg and setting up to hit the ball aggressively into the net.

My team cheered as the Ref blew three whistles, the game ending with us on top of a tight 2-1 match up. Despite the fact it wasn't my goal, I shook the goalie's hand, before jogging up the field to meet the rest of the girls. Liv tackled me to the ground, giggling the whole time.

"You killed it!" I told her, "Your shots are always top-notch."

"Thanks," she laughed. "And thank you for the *top-notch* assist."

"Alright girls off the ground," Coach Terry said, "It's not enough to play like professionals, we need to look it too."

Liv and I stood, attempting to rub off the grass stains that now decorated the edges of our shorts. The rest of our teammates gathered around Coach in a circle, offering us pats of congratulations along the way. Terry squat down on the balls of her feet, and the rest of us followed suit, as she pulled out her clipboard to go over the notes of today's game. As always, there was never a simple, "congrats, you did a good job now go enjoy your afternoon." It was a half hour of critiques, analysis, and what we could do better. But afterwards, when we all stood to leave, Terry stopped us and said she had news.

"As you all know, the biggest tournament of the year in our division is Maydel," she said; Liv shot me a look. "I would like to inform you that our team has been applied. I didn't want to say anything until things were in the works, but we made it past the first round of application, so I thought it was time you knew. This was our toughest competition so far and coming off of this win I would say that chances are high as long as you keep on a winning streak. Either way, I should know by the end of this week. You may go now and I'll see you for practice Monday."

The team dispersed. Liv and I began to turn away together when Terry called our names. We both looked back, and followed, as she pulled us away a few feet.

"What's up?" Liv asked.

"I've been watching you two," Terry said. "Both good players and good teammates, you work well together. If Maydel happens, I'll want team captains leading us forward. Hypothetically, I would like to know the interest of you both. I would expect a continuing prioritization of this team and this team alone. You would be MVP players and leaders for your teammates. Obviously, this is only if and when, we receive word on the tournament. But, as I deliver an answer to the team on that, I would also like to deliver our captains. So, what do you say?"

"What do we say? Of course!" Liv jumped. "You can count on us."

"Excellent," Terry said, "We'll talk later this week." As soon as Terry had walked away, Liv turned to me with a gleeful smile.

"Can you believe it?" she asked, "This is perfect, the exact scenario we always talked about!"

"Don't get too excited, it isn't for sure yet," I emphasized. "Besides,

I'm pretty sure I could have answered for myself, thank you very much."

"Oh please, what's the harm?" she asked, "I knew you were gonna say yes, I mean why wouldn't you?"

"Well it is a big commitment," I said, "It would have to be my number one priority."

"So? It already is! I mean, what could be more important than this?"

10

I watched as Hope charged across the field. She flew by the defenders and tapped the ball to the side, just as I would have, before shooting it into the lower left corner of the goal. I jumped and cheered from the sidelines as Hope ran along the line to give me a high five before returning to her spot on the field.

By the end of the game, Hope had scored a second, and was playing better than I'd ever seen her. She came off the field with a big smile and met me for another high five. I handed her her water, and together we walked back to the check-in desk, where her family would be waiting to pick her up. Pete was already talking with them by the time we got over, telling them all about her great performance in the group game. Hope blushed at their proud faces as they signed to her excitedly. Once they were done, Pete took a step back as the parents touched Hope's shoulder to indicate it was time to leave. Hope hesitated and turned to me, she fiddled her fingers with clear frustration, then gave in and signed to Pete. Pete smiled and looked back at me.

"She wants to say thank you and that she had a great time," he said.

I smiled at her gratefully and nodded my head, she came in and gave me a quick hug before turning quickly to leave. Her parents smiled and squeezed each other's hands as they followed her out. Warmth spread in my heart and I smiled at the promise of a continuing friendship.

11

"It's happening!" Liv practically screamed in my face as she walked into history later that week.

"What's happening?" I asked as she swiveled her body from where she now sat on my desk.

"Maydel! What else?" she beamed.

"No way!" I said.

"Yes way!" she cheered, "I'm so excited!"

"Wait, how do you know?" I asked. "We haven't had practice yet and I haven't heard anything."

"That's cause Coach is gonna announce it at practice tonight!"

"Okay, but that still doesn't answer how you know," I pointed out.

"True," she said, "I ran into Terry last night when I was at dinner with my dad, she told me that she wanted the two of us to know in advance, cause of the whole captain's thing, and that she was gonna call last night to tell us anyway. . . so she just told me! I told her that I'd tell you today so everything was set! What kind of crazy luck is that?"

"Pretty crazy," I said.

"Why aren't you more excited?" she asked.

"I am, believe me, I am, I guess I just didn't expect for us to hear on it so soon, but here we are! It's gonna be great," I smiled.

*   *   *

That afternoon, Liv was practically quaking with anticipation; it was driving her crazy to keep quiet about the tournament. I watched as she was about ready to explode by the end of practice, just in time for Terry to pull everyone aside for "season updates".

"Alright ladies, we have some things to go over," Terry said with non-existent enthusiasm. "First of all, I am pleased to inform you all that we are one of the selected teams to partake in the Maydel tournament this season." She paused all we all poked each other and squealed with excitement. "Second, before you all start a race for MVP, I have already chosen the captains for this tournament, I approached them, and they both accepted. That being said, Liv and Nadia please come forward."

As I walked to the front, I noticed that the girl's faces held a mixture of respect and jealousy, and they weren't quite split the way I would have hoped.

"These two girls will be your team captains for the rest of this season, they have both displayed great strength both on and off the field, and have great instincts when it comes to each other, which will be especially helpful when making coupled decisions on team matters. Coming off of that, my last bit of information is a change in schedule. Yes, we will continue with our standard days of practice, but we are also adding a day, and that will be Sunday--" My heart stopped as I waited to hear time. "These practices will run from 4 to 5:30 and they will be entirely run by your captains. I will be present for observation, but that is all. Liv and Nadia have already been informed of the expected commitment on their end, and I will continue to watch as to make sure that does not fall through," she said sternly. "That is all for now, as you know we have a bi-weekend on games so you have tomorrow off, make use of it, you won't be having another for a while."

As our teammates started leaving, Liv and I made our way to our bikes.

"We get to run our own captain practices!" Liv said, "I've heard of those before but didn't think they did them in our age group."

"It seems pretty unusual, and don't you think it's a little weird that she never talked to us about it before, and just went and announced it to the whole team?" I asked, bending down to unlock my bike.

"I take it as a sign of trust," Liv said, "She knows we can do it."

"I know, a little warning just would have been nice. I was really worried she was going to say it was at the same time as VIP. That would have been a disaster," I said, buckling my helmet.

"What's the difference whether it's at the same time or right after?" Liv asked, "It's not like you can keep doing it either way."

"Why?" I asked.

"Because, we're gonna have way too much going on with our own team, you shouldn't be wasting your energy on somebody else's." Liv threw her leg over her bike and was ready to get on her way, "Besides, if you go to VIP before, you'll be all tired coming into our practice, and won't play as well," she said, "It's just not worth it."

12

I had just slipped on my buddy shirt, when I heard a knock at the door. My mom wasn't home so I ran across the house to look out the window before opening it. I was surprised to find Liv standing there, backpack slouched over her shoulder. I opened the door, and she smiled, immediately walking inside before saying a word.

"Hey Liv, what's up? I don't have much time before I have to go," I said, moving to grab my water from the kitchen table.

"Go where?" she asked, walking into the living room and sprawling herself on my couch.

"VIP," I said, "It's starts in a half hour and I have to bike, so I can't talk long."

"I thought we talked about this," Liv said with annoyance, "The fact you can't do both."

"No," I said, "You talked about it. I decided that I *could* do both."

"Come on," Liv said, pulling her body up from the cushions. "We have to plan for practice tonight. If we show up unprepared, it'll look super bad," she tilted her head and touched my hand, "For the team."

*   *   *

That night, I found myself lying on my bed, exhausted. I hadn't played any longer than usual, our practice was the same length. But somehow, the combination of practice, and the planning hours with Liv, had taken the desire out of me. I had time before dinner, it was a weekend so I didn't have homework, there was nothing special going on, and yet, I didn't want to get back on the field. I wasn't anticipating the next night with my team, I wasn't restless with a desire to practice more. I was content, just lying there, doing nothing.

"Nadia!" I heard my mom call from the kitchen. Slowly, I lifted my body from the bed and sauntered across the house to meet her. As I came around the corner, I watched as she slipped the landline back into its holster. When my footsteps echoed a mere few feet from her, she turned to face me.

"Yeah?" I asked.

"Pete just called," she said, arms crossed. "You didn't go to VIP today?"

"Um," I shuffled my feet, "Well, no."

"Any reason?" she asked, clearly irritated from my lack of explanation.

"Well, Liv came over right as I was gonna leave. She was all stressed cause we hadn't made plans for the captain's practice yet, and she felt like there wasn't time for me to do both," I kept my eyes on the ground. "So, I decided to skip it to help her. Are you mad?"

"Nadia, if you can't go to every practice that's okay. I'm not mad you couldn't go today, I'm upset that you didn't care to mention it to me, or better yet, Pete, who was standing at the front table with Hope, waiting for you. When you didn't show, without a word, he was afraid something was wrong. That's the second time he had tried to call me, just to make sure everything was okay."

"I'm sorry, I just didn't think about it, it was so last minute and I didn't think it would even matter. Sorry."

"It's okay," my mom took my face in her hands, "But if that happens again, no matter how last minute, you need to promise me you'll do the responsible thing, and tell us."

"I would, but, um," I continued looking at the ground, "I don't think it'll really matter . . ."

"What do you mean by that?" my mom asked.

"I'm not gonna do VIP anymore."

"What? Why?" my mom asked with surprise. "You were so happy after last week, and Pete said you and Hope were really bonding."

"I know, and we were," I stumbled. "But I think Liv's right, I just don't have enough time, I need to focus on my own team, not someone else's."

"Are those your words, or Liv's?" she asked, leaning her elbows on the counter. I didn't respond, averting my eyes.

"You don't have to decide right this second," my mom continued, "And whatever you decide is okay, just make sure it's your decision."

She kissed my forehead before walking to the cabinet to gather some spices. I turned to leave, when she said one last thing over her shoulder.

"But Nadia, if you do decide to stop VIP, promise me one thing."

"Yeah?"

"According to Pete, Hope was very sad, and not herself, when you didn't show up. It probably didn't help that there was no explanation as to why. So, promise me, if you aren't going to do it anymore, that you will go there yourself, and let her know. She deserves that much."

I bit my lip at the subtle sting of my heart.

"I promise."

13

"I think Jenna should be our sweeper for the tournament, what about you?" Liv asked from the seat beside me as our teacher droned on about Charlemagne.

"What?" I raised a brow.

"Maydel, Jenna, Sweeper, yes?"

"I mean yeah if she wants, she's good, but why are you even thinking about that right now?"

"Because it's not what *she* wants, or what they want, it's what *we* want, we're the captains!" Liv said just loud enough for the teacher to grant us a look of irritation. Liv offered a soft apology smile before turning right back to me, awaiting a response.

"Exactly, we're captains, not coaches," I clarified, "Leave some decisions to Terry."

"I'm just trying to help our team, why are you being so rude?"

"I'm not trying to be, I guess I just don't understand why this has to be our everything," I said.

"What do you mean? Why don't you get it? This is important. To me, to our team, and I thought to you," Liv slid in with edge.

"I know it's important to you Liv," I pleaded, "And yes it's important to me too, but some things are more important."

Some things are more important, I repeated in my head.

*   *   *

That night, back at my house, I watched the minutes tick by, meanwhile downing sips of an energy drink, and biting bits off a chocolate bar, in an attempt to keep my eyelids from fluttering closed. Finally, the clock's little hand crept past midnight, and as it was 11 am for my sister, it was her break time for the day, and the only time calls were allowed if they weren't pre-arranged.

I picked up the phone and connected to the overseas line. Waiting as the beeps went in and out until finally, I heard a click on the other end.

"Hello?" I heard my sister's voice, clearly without knowledge of who had called her.

"Lesya," I said.

"Nadia," she responded; I could hear her smile through the phone, "How are you?"

"Good," I shifted in my seat on the bed.

"Yeah right," she said back immediately, "I can tell that's not true and you know it, so spill."

"Well," I started. "My team got into this huge tournament, the biggest in the state, and on top of that, Liv and I were chosen as co-captains. I'm super excited about it and all, it's just that doing both VIP and the team right now, isn't working out so well, especially with our added practices," I rambled on. "Liv thinks I should quit VIP all together but when I skipped one of the practices, mom and Pete were both upset I didn't tell them, and from what they said, Hope's upset too. I should be really happy, but everything just feels like a mess right now. I don't know how to please everyone. I don't know what to do."

"Nadia, take a breath, you're stressed and over-analyzing," Lesya said with her typical calm demeanor. "First of all, you can't please everyone, you never can, so stop trying to. Work on pleasing yourself and what makes you feel good. Now, you can quit or you can try to do both, what are your thoughts?"

"Well, Liv thinks that me doing both is taking away from our team which is a commitment I made before VIP," I explained.

"I didn't ask what Liv thought," Lesya pointed out, "I know how Liv feels about it, I want to know about you."

"I think, that I thought it was going to be easy to ditch VIP and go back to my team, and just my team. And agreeing to stay with her, and skip a practice was my choice not hers, and I was fine with it. Or I thought I was, until I heard that Pete called mom and said how sad Hope was. I wasn't expecting to hear that and I wasn't expecting it to hurt."

"Mmhm," Lesya murmured, "And why do you think it hurts?"

"Maybe I care about VIP more than I thought?" I wondered.

"Only you can know that for sure," she said softly. "Hey, someone just came in to the clinic so I have to go, whatever you do, promise it's for you, and you won't talk to Liv, or mom, or anyone, until you've decided."

"I promise," I said.

"Listen to your gut, it's gotten you this far," Lesya said. "I love you."

"Wait, Lesya," I intervened, "When you said I could quit, did you mean VIP or the team?"

"Does it matter?" she asked immediately before clicking off.

"Love you too," I whispered after the dial tone went blank.

*   *   *

As I lay in my bed that night, I somehow lost my earlier desire for sleep. I couldn't stop relaying Lesya's question in my mind, *does it matter?* I had always thought my choice was between figuring out both, or forgetting VIP. I had never considered quitting my own team an option. I wasn't having fun like I used to, but did that mean I didn't care about it at all anymore? Lesya had always put others before herself, was it time for me to do that too? But the people I loved were pulling me in such different directions, how could I possibly know which way to go? And can you truly help others, if you haven't helped yourself first?

And just like that, I became so exhausted with my own thought, that I slept deeper than I had in months.

14

Biking to VIP that weekend, I felt sure about my decision. I could do both. I didn't have to give either up, it was all about balance. As I locked my bike by the curb of the parking lot, and crossed the grasses to the check in desk, Pete stood to face me.

"Glad to have you back," he said, patting my shoulder, "And I think someone else is too," he pointed behind me.

I turned to see Hope coming up to us, a big smile on her face. I smiled back and waved before she ran up to give me a hug. I was caught off guard by her reaction, but it warmed by heart. I motioned for her to walk with me, and together we went and started pumping up some game balls. As we sat across from each other, legs beneath us, I saw that she was wearing a heart-shaped locket inscribed with her initials. I smiled and she looked at me questioningly. I pointed at myself, then gave a thumbs up, pointed at her, and reached to my chest, indicating, as best I could, that I liked her necklace. She seemed to understand, and did the same motions, but referencing my bracelet. I blushed, looking down at Lesya's name, knowing she would be proud that I was sitting there.

As practice went on I could tell that, despite my absence, Hope had been working hard this past week. She seemed excited to show me, and I noticed how she had perfected her dribbling, weaving in and out of cones effortlessly. I smiled, and clapped for her, when she turned back to me. Then, she stepped in front of the ball; assuming it was her showing she was done, I stood, ready to walk towards her. But then, she took her left foot, ran the ball over her right calf and flipped it up perfectly to land in the grass before her.

I gaped in amazement. The rainbow? I couldn't believe she had learned it so fast. She was upset that I hadn't shown up last week, but instead of pouting, she used it to work harder and learn more. She didn't know if I would be back, it wasn't for me, it was for her, her own perseverance. I hadn't seen that kind of discipline at such a young age in anyone but Lesya. I felt my eyes water a little but I shook it off, surprised by my own reaction, but I don't think Hope noticed. She beamed at my impressment and kicked the ball to my feet, sassily expecting me to respond with my own rainbow. I laughed and rolled the ball beneath my feet before attempting the rainbow myself, but I was off kilter. The ball went sideways instead of straight. I was embarrassed and grabbed it immediately in my hands, shrugging. Hope shook her head and put it at my feet. I looked at her with surprise, but she pointed at it again and I found myself repeating the action, only this time I did it right. I looked up and Hope nodded, I smiled and laughed at myself. I guess I had more than one thing to learn from her.

* * *

At the end of practice, after Hope and the other kids had left, I found myself following Tadd around with a netted bag, ready to receive cones as he picked them off the field.

"You and Hope really seem to be getting somewhere," he noted. "That's awesome. You guys match up well, she really seems to like you."

"I like her too, she's a little spitfire," I laughed, "I never knew how sassy you could be without words."

"She's been teaching you a lot then?" he asked.

"Yeah," I pondered, "She really has."

"And I know you've taught her a lot," he encouraged.

"I don't know about a lot," I said, "I hope some. Anyway, I really just wish I could communicate better with her, some things are just easier expressed with words."

"Well, I'm sure you can come up with some way to do that," he said, "You seem pretty smart."

"Thanks."

"But hey, off topic, but I know I told you a few weeks back that I like to do these pick-up games, that Keller and I both do. I think you'd have a lot of fun playing too, if you're interested?"

"Are you inviting me?" I asked.

"What are friends for?" he said.

"I'll try it, why not," I said, starting to walk away; then over my shoulder, "Looking forward to scoring on you!"

"We'll see about that," he snapped back.

As I made my way to my bike, I saw that Pete hadn't left yet, he was still packing up some supplies in his car. As he shut the trunk and rounded to the front seat, I jogged up to cut him off.

"Hey, Pete!"

"Nadia, what can I do for you?"

"Um, I was just wondering, on my first day you had told me about a class you took to learn sign language . . . any chance I could take it too?"

15

"Good morning students, glad to see a mix of old and new faces. For those who are new, my name is Professor Silmin. Thank you for your interest in American Sign Language and welcome to our class."

I adjusted my position on the chair, a mixed feeling of nervousness and excitement overtaking me. Pete had helped me sign up for the class, *ASL 101,* at the local community college, open to all ages. He was now in the secondary class, as he had reached a point of being conversational in sign. If all goes as planned, I will come to the hour-long class a few days a week and get to a point where I am conversational in a matter of months. It even worked out to start after my soccer practice, after practice and before dinner, the perfect pocket of time. I twiddled a pen between my fingers nervously, everything appeared to be working out, I only worried it would be short-lived.

*   *   *

By the end of my first class, I knew how to count to twenty, introduce myself, say hello, good-bye, please and thank you. Biking home, I pictured myself walking up to Hope next practice and confidently introducing myself in a way she would understand. I could even ask my Professor at the next class how to tell her that my name means hope, to make it even better. I would go to two more classes by the end of the weekend, who knows what I will have learned by then. She would be so impressed, the same way I was with her rainbow at practice yesterday. The thought excited me, but as I pondered it more, I realized that I wanted to wait until the following practice, wait until I know, and understand, a little more rather than get ahead of myself. It would be a better surprise if I would wait just a little longer.

As I walked through my side gate, I could already smell the thick spices my mom was undoubtedly stirring at the stove. I heard her soft voice chattering as I came into the kitchen and saw her smiling into the phone, leaned against the counter. She gave me a little wave, and spoke into the phone: "Your sister just walked in," she said, "No, she wasn't at practice, she was, actually I'll let her tell you," she took the phone off her ear and reached it toward me. "I'm going to need it back in a few minutes but I'm sure she'd like to hear from you," she told me.

"Thanks," I said.

"How was it?" she whispered as I brought the phone up to my ear. I gave her a thumbs up as I said hi to Lesya on my way out the room.

"So," she said, "Mom wouldn't tell me where you were. . . it must be a big deal."

"Yeah, it was pretty cool."

"Well, tell me!" she cried; I laughed.

"Actually," I said, "I was in class. A sign language class," I smiled.

"Really? Nadia, that's amazing! What'd you think?"

"It was pretty awesome," I admitted. "It's interesting, the Professor started teaching us some things at the end, but the first half, he did an overview on the class and I guess every few days we'll have a 'culture-class', where we learn more about the culture of sign. I had no idea the ASL community was so large."

"Yeah, it really is incredible, I've learned a bit about sign culture since being overseas, they have a really empowering sense of community. I think we could all learn from it . . . so what made you decide to take the class?"

"Hope did something at practice that required a lot of dedication, and effort, and I guess I just thought maybe I should do the same," I said shyly, I hadn't even thought about why I was asking Pete when I did, I just knew that I should.

"Well, I'm very proud of you, I think it's great," she expressed.

"Thanks," I said. "How are you? How are things going?"

"Same old, same old," she laughed, "Which is both good and bad I guess." I was about to ask her what she meant when I heard my mom calling;

"Nadia!" she said, "Can you bring me the phone, I need to ask Lesya something."

"Hey, mom's asking for you," I said.

"Yeah I heard," she laughed, "She's always seemed to think that our walls are a lot thicker than they are." *Our walls,* I couldn't remember the last time I heard Lesya say anything reflecting that she still thought of this place as home.

"Can't deny that," I responded, joining in her laughter, then getting up to return the phone to my mom. "We'll talk again soon, yeah?"

"Of course," she smiled, "I can't wait to hear more, love you."

"Love you too," I said, "Stay safe." Then dropping the phone to my side as I walked back into the kitchen.

16

At practice the next day, it felt like I didn't even get to play at all. I spent the whole time running around with Liv, telling other people what to do, where to go, and what to change. Terry stood nearby with watchful eyes, observing our every move.

"Hey, ever feel like you're being watched?" Liv rolled her eyes; I smiled,

"Yeah and for some reason, it always seems to be at this park." We both laughed, which took enough time away from the game for Terry to have a problem.

"I'm not sure why soccer would be so funny, girls," she said, dragging out the last word as though its utterance was somehow an insult.

We both looked at each other quickly, then separated to monitor different teammates. We had one group doing a passing weave drill and another practicing shooting. We had five cones spread across the field where each player would run in and out, one at a time, to work different angles.

During the next water break, Liv looked at her watch and saw that there were only twenty minutes left in the practice. "Scrimmage?" she looked up to me, I nodded excitedly. "Cool with you Coach?" she turned to Terry for the final approval.

"Yeah, I think you guys have earned it," she said, I felt a wave of relief wash over me, finally I would actually get to play. Terry picked a netted bag from the trunk of her car and started passing out pennies. "Nadia, red, Liv, green," she said as she threw the differing colors equally among our teammates. Liv and I took to the field with our pennie-mates and began working out positions when Terry walked over and shut us down.

"You two aren't playing," she said, "You're coaching, on the sidelines," she pointed across the way.

"Why?" I asked.

"You need to learn your team, watching and instructing will make you better players," she explained.

"Playing would make us better players," I said with a little more edge than I intended. She raised a brow at me then pointed with more defiance,

"On the sideline!" she shouted. Liv and I both ducked our heads and scurried off the field.

"You better watch what you say, she did not look happy," Liv warned.

I shook my head to myself, I may not stand by the tone I used, but I stand by what I said. Playing is how you get to be a better player, if it was up to me, practice would be constant scrimmage.

After Terry blew the whistle to end the game, we all jogged off the field and gathered to grab our belongings and head out, but she stopped us with an announcement.

"I'm inputting an additional practice tomorrow," she said, "An all-drill practice," giving me a side-eye glance. "Be here at 7 o'clock."

Tomorrow, at seven, that was the exact time I was supposed to be meeting Tadd and Keller at the park across town for their pick-up game. Ignoring my better judgement, I raised my hand slightly and looked at Terry;

"I can't be there tomorrow," I said. She looked me in the eye with great irritation, but refrained from responding, merely ignoring me to turn back to the team.

"Be here tomorrow at seven," she repeated, then turned to leave.

17

The next day was a whirlwind of school, homework, ASL class, cooking dinner with my mom, and now, biking to my first ever pick-up game of soccer. I wound through the park and trees at an increasing speed, eager to get there. It took place at Ginnen Park, one I had never been to before. I crossed under a bridge scattered with graffiti of all colors and design; other bikers rode by easily, strolling their way out of the park. Once I came out of the shadow of the bridge, I looked up to see a beautiful stretch of green with a few oak trees scattered here and there, even a small duck pond tucked in on the right, and dotted with stepping stones.

I found myself smiling as the breeze tugged at my ponytail, everything just felt so peaceful. As the path wound slightly to the left, I saw the first promise of a soccer game. A few people across the field, passing the ball and greeting friends with each incoming arrival. I peeled my eyes for a familiar face until I noticed Keller off to the side, chatting with another girl and sipping Gatorade. I rode for another dozen yards before flipping my leg over my bike, and walking it the rest of the way. I looked for a bike rack, but didn't see one, Keller caught my eye and waved me over. With one arm still flung over the handlebar, I said hi and shook her friend's hand.

"Melanie," she said.

"Nadia," I introduced myself; then realizing I was still hanging on my bike. "Hey, is there somewhere I can lock this up?"

"You don't need to lock it," Keller said, "We're all friends here, leave it anywhere."

"Okay," I said, moving another few yards away to park it on the other side of the path. "So, how does this work?" I asked.

"We play," Keller laughed, "That's about it."

"Are there cones or anything for the sidelines?" I asked.

"Nah, we go wherever we wanna go," I heard a voice, "If the ball's in play, it's in play." I turned to see that Tadd had arrived and walked up behind me.

"Hey!" I said.

"Glad you could make it," he smiled, "Keller, Melanie." They both responded with sups and dude. I watched as a girl and a guy walked to the center and called everyone up. "Jane and Louis," Tadd clarified, "They're a couple, and the ones who started this tradition, wanted a more effective way to compete against each other," he laughed.

"Today we're gonna use those two trees as one goal and the bushes as the other," Jane said, then cutting between the center of the group, "If you're on my left you're the bush team, and on my right, the tree team," she said, then flipping back around, "Everyone good?"

There were murmurs of agreement between the crowd before the parting began as people split off from each other to head to their respective side. I found myself on the same side as both Keller and Melanie, who apparently were a sweeper/stopper team, immediately heading to the back side of the field. I looked to Tadd, who was the cut off line for the opposite team.

"You're a forward right?" he asked, raising a brow.

"Naturally," I said. "And you?"

"Oh please, you already know I'm a keeper," he stuck out his tongue at his own joke and put his arms in the air as he backed over to the trees.

"Perfect," I said, arms crossed over my chest.

Once I got to the imaginary mid-line, I introduced myself to the other forwards and, as I was the center, when Louis walked over to pick the starting team, I was the one who had to make the guess. The team's center was a boy about my age, unlike most of the other people here, with curly brown hair, tight on his scalp. Louis stood in front of us and held both arms behind his back.

"How many fingers?" he asked, "Tree team?"

"Eight," the boy responded.

"Bush team?"

"Seven."

"It was seven, bush team it is," he dropped the ball at my feet and moved back to his position on the tree team at center-mid.

"Ready?" he called from his line, "One, two, three, play!"

I touched the ball gently to my right, where the next girl picked it up and immediately rolled it to the side, bolting up her line. Louis and one of the other midfielders crowded her, and in desperation, she kicked the ball to the middle. I was about to dodge in when the tree team's stopper jumped forward and slammed the ball back to our defense. Keller got to it first and I watched as she pointed me towards the center before delivering an expertly arched kick to land right in the sweet spot of the field. I ran with it, taking it up into a dribble without stopping, and softly moved it to the side when a defender leapt in front of me. I felt pressure from another player gaining speed on me, they were trying to run me down the line. I looked across to see one of the other forwards, mimicking my paces, at center field. I crossed him the ball and he took it up the center, his speed outweighing that of the other players. He charged toward the goal and, when the sweeper came at him from twenty feet out, he wailed the ball into the far-right corner, impossibly out of Tadd's reach.

We cheered and ran back to the midline, exchanging high fives and pats on the back. We were now in the lead. But when the game started again, the Tree Team came back angry, they charged forward, full-force, pushing back our line until we were just before the goal. Their striker slammed a hard shot just over the goal. Our keeper went to retrieve it and brought it about 15 feet in front of the goal, kicking it up all the way to the midline, but apparently it wasn't quite far enough, one of the Tree Team's midfielders, chested the ball, hit it up on her knee and then let it fall to the top of her foot, wailing it up the field, an impressive, and lucky, volley that cost us a goal.

We continued back and forth, scoreless, equally pitted against each other with a see-saw of close calls. With only a few minutes left in the first half, I sent the ball up the field to a fellow forward. Directly placed between them, and the defense.

They did a quick scissors move to avoid the line and I thought we had a chance, within seconds they made a beautiful shot to the lower left corner, but Tadd dove expertly and caught it just in time for them to blow the whistle, signaling halftime.

As I sipped my water, Tadd came up to me, shaking his head.

"You got something to say?" I said sassily.

"You're good," he said.

"Thanks," I smiled.

"But, I'm still pretty disappointed," he admitted.

"Why's that?" I asked, unsure of whether or not he was joking.

"Because, you're holding back, and I have a feeling you always do," he analyzed me.

"What do you mean I'm holding back? You don't think I was playing well?"

"I think you were playing very well, for someone who doesn't want to score," he noted.

"Well, that's a little offensive," I said, hand on hip.

"I don't mean it that way," he said. "It's just, I get not wanting to be a ball hog, but you give the ball away every chance you get. Don't get me wrong, you give it away very well, and often resulting in assists, but sometimes it's your turn to score. Obviously if someone is in a better position than you, give them the shot, but if you can, and you have the ball, then keep going, take it. I may not want you to score on me, but I do want you to shoot on me," he winked, heading over to talk to Louis.

I found myself searching in my mind, looking back to when I had last taken a real shot in a game. I had assisted almost every goal we'd had all season, but none for myself. I pondered this for a minute, but before long, it was time to re-start the game. I made my way back over to the midline, and this time, it was the Tree Team's turn to start.

The game continued on without a change to the score and we were almost to the end. I had one opportunity, but like Tadd said, I found myself giving the ball away, without any thought, it was automatic, like clockwork. More back and forth until the Tree Team got their second goal and I knew there were only a few minutes left. As we stood at the midline and the ball was passed to me, I knew this was my opportunity. I took the ball up the field.

One by one, I ran the thread through their defense, until it was just me and Tadd. A few feet from the goal, he made the best move he could, lunging at my feet for the ball. As fast as it all felt, my mind swam circles and I knew how I wanted to avoid his advance. I curled the ball under my foot, up my calf and flicked my feet so perfectly, that the ball didn't even need a second kick, it went straight into the net. Tadd was already on the ground, but when he heard the swish, he looked up in amazement, and then at me with pride, as the final whistle blew.

"That's what I like to see, and glad she got to see too," he smiled, pointing across the line. I gazed out until my eyes reached the bike path, where I saw an outline of Hope, watching the game.

"You told her to come?" I asked.

"Yup," he said, standing up and wiping at the grass stains, "Thought she needed to see you play for real."

"But you didn't know for sure that I was coming," I reminded him.

"Please, I haven't even seen you with your team and I know you're over it just by the way you talk about it. But what you're not over, is soccer, and this kind of stuff is the heart of soccer. You weren't gonna miss a chance to play," he winked before jogging off to catch up with some of the others. Leaving me to go greet Hope, on my own.

As I walked toward her, she smiled and waved, I did the same back. I wanted so badly to show her what I had learned in sign class, but at the same time, I wanted to wait.

I stood there uncomfortably for a few minutes, not sure what to do in this setting. Not yet able to talk with words, but nothing to try and accomplish without words. But Hope's smirk spoke for me, she pulled a ball from the sideline, and did a perfect rainbow. She smiled over her shoulder and gestured for me to follow as she started dribbling toward center field. I laughed and chased after her, nothing to do but play the game.

18

I climbed off my bike and pulled my soccer bag down off my shoulder, unzipping the front pocket to retrieve my water bottle. As I took a few sips, I scanned the fields for my team. I spotted them gathering across the way, adjusted my shin guards, and jogged over to where they stood. By the time I got over there, my teammates were just starting the first warm-up drill. I let the bag slide off my shoulder, ready to dump it and join them, but Terry stopped me.

"Not you," she said, merely sticking her pen out in front of me and not bothering to look up from her clipboard.

"What do you mean, not me?" I asked, trying not to be irritated.

"You didn't attend the *mandatory* practice on Thursday," she said pointedly.

"I told you I couldn't make it," I said.

"I didn't tell you it was okay," she snapped back. "You're running laps until the start of the game."

"What?" I looked at my watch, "But that's not for 45 minutes! That's a workout, not a warm-up. I'll already be tired before the game even starts."

"Well, then maybe it'll get you into better shape," Terry said rudely as I hugged my pre-pubescent body.

"What about helping out with coaching?" I asked quietly, trying to hide my newfound self-consciousness.

"Liv can handle it," she said simply. "And if you want to stay a captain with her, then I would suggest you stop asking questions, focus on this team, and do as I say, now, laps!" she said, for the first time looking up from the clipboard and only to flash me a look of anger.

I turned away without saying anything else, and jogged off as though I didn't care, but as I ran the corner of the first lap, I felt a silent tear fall from the corner of my left eye.

*　　　*　　　*

The sun was beginning to beat down, and I felt my skin growing sweaty in the heat. The ref called captains to the centerfield and I went into a sprint trying to reach them, but Terry had already sent Liv without me. She didn't even acknowledge me when I stopped short at the team tent, but continued to bark out instructions until Liv got back to grant the news that we'd be kicking off. Terry picked right back up to go over the game's line-up, she went back to front calling out names fluidly, but once she reached the frontline, she paused. I watched as she lifted her pen and made an adjustment to her paper before reading off the final three names, and mine wasn't one of them. The whole team seemed to look up in surprise, I was always a starter. Liv looked over at me and opened her mouth as though to say something, but before she could, Terry broke the silence,

"Everyone on the field!" she called out.

Everyone but me, I thought. I bit my lip as I paced alongside the tent with arms crossed, Terry ignored me. I debated whether to ignore or confront, but when I looked up to see my teammate Leela, standing in my position, ball at her feet, waiting for the ref's whistle, my frustration deepened.

"Why are you doing this?" I asked with more defeat than anger. "I ran laps right up until the game started, I missed one practice, and I told you beforehand that I couldn't go. I'm always a starter, you picked me as captain because you saw me as a team MVP. So why am I sitting on the sidelines?"

"You said that you would be tired before the game starts, so you'll sit out the first quarter because apparently you haven't been doing enough running training. Now if you'll excuse me, I have a team to coach." She turned so forcefully that her ponytail whipped from one to shoulder to the other, slapping her cheek in the process, before stepping away from the tent, and toward the center line.

I closed my eyes and took a deep breath, slowly taking a seat on the team bench, accepting my loss. The smell of fresh cut grass drifted, the breeze tugged at the netting on the goal post, 9 v 9 across the field,

18 thirteen-year-old girls crouched, stacked against each other. Complete silence in the last moment. The game was about to start.

I buried my face in my hands and silently groaned under my breath. I couldn't understand how I had gone from being Terry's "golden-girl" less than a week ago, to here, where I faltered once from what she wanted, and suddenly, everything I did and said was wrong. I looked up as the first whistle blew. The other team immediately snatched the ball from our forward line and kicked it up to our defense. It was torture to watch them play. The game that I love, the thing I was best at, the thing I had worked so hard for, but as I sat there on the sidelines, it felt like that thing was slipping away from me.

At the end of the game, my mom was helping me put my bike in her car, when she attempted to casually ask what was going on with me and Terry.

"I just want to play, and I skipped one day of drills to do just that, and now, it's like I'm not even a member of the team anymore."

She knew not to ask anything else, just to get in the car with me, and drive home. Radio on, letting me drown out my thoughts.

Once in the house, my mom made her way to our computer to check email as I immediately headed to my room, only stopping to pluck the phone from the extension in the kitchen. I shut my door and fell onto my bed, as another silent tear left a streak across my cheek. I ran a hand through my greasy hair, not caring that I hadn't showered and knowing the dirt and sweat I would be leaving behind on the comforter. I turned the phone on its side, and punched in the numbers, giving information when needed and waiting for that dial tone. As it finally clicked on, I heard a groggy voice at the end,

"Hello?" Lesya said, clearing not yet awake.

"It's Nadia," I said quietly, guilty for not considering the time change.

"How are you?" she asked, immediately perking up.

"I don't want to talk about me," I said, "Tell me how you are."

I lay there on my bed, curled to the side, listening to my sister tell her story for once, all the things she's seen and had to do, and all without a single complaint. *This is what I signed up for, it was my choice,* her words echoed in my head.

19

The next day, I woke up ready to pretend like yesterday never happened. I went about my regular day until it was time to for VIP. I pulled on the red buddy shirt, grabbed a water bottle on my way out, and practically skipped to the side-gate where I'd left my bike. It was as though yesterday had made me more eager to be around the game, rather than less. My mom was noticeably confused about my upbeat attitude, but refrained from questioning. I waved through the window on my way out, she returned it with a smile that may as well have been a laugh.

As I wove through the bike paths, I closed my eyes and inhaled the scent of fresh jasmine. The sun's rays were comforting, like a warm outstretching hug. I slowed my bike and hit the brakes when I reached the parking lot; walking it the rest of the way to the racks. When I looked up the hill, it was empty. I glanced down at my watch, twenty minutes until the start of practice. I walked over slowly, arms holding each other, when I thought I heard something coming from the club building across the field. I searched to find the sound's source, until I came across an open side door and walked in to find Pete, watching an old video reel.

On it, I saw a young Pete, holding the hand of an even younger boy. Together they walked, then ran, across an open field. The clip faded and another came up, on the same field, this time with a ball. The same drill, walking, then running, side by side, but with the ball between them. The boy was clearly using Pete for assistance, but you would never know by the smile on his face. I found myself smiling back at him when I shifted in my stance causing a mild clang against the tile floors. Pete turned to see me still standing in the doorway, my cheeks flushed.

"Sorry, I just, I didn't mean to, sorry," I stuttered, turning to leave.

"Nadia," he said, "Please, come in, I don't mind."

"Okay," I said, "Sorry, I was just a little early today."

"I guess I could say the same," he smiled. "Sometimes it's nice to be early, you have more time to appreciate what you're doing."

I nodded quietly, fixating my gaze on the paused still of Pete and the boy, waving at the camera.

"My brother," he said, as though reading my thoughts. "And the reason I started this program."

"What was wrong with him? Or wait, no, sorry, that came out wrong. Nothing's wrong with him, or anyone else," I shook my head, "I guess, I just mean, why were you helping him?"

"He had down syndrome," Pete said.

"Had?" I asked.

"Yes, unfortunately he passed away a few years ago. He always loved soccer. I started thinking about this program over a decade ago, but it was his passing, that finally got me to do it," he explained.

"I'm so sorry," I said quietly.

"Thank you," he said with a glazed look in his eye. "His name was Noah, but I always called him Viper because he was always moving, always sneaking up on me. That's where I got the name VIP."

I pondered that for a moment, realizing that I had never bothered, or even thought, to ask where it got its name. It had never crossed my mind. I started to wonder how many other things I had overlooked in the same way.

"Well, enough on me," he cleared his throat, "How are you? Are you enjoying your ASL class?"

"I actually am," I said. "It's really interesting. I feel like I'm learning a lot, but, at the same time, I feel helpless, like I don't even know how to ask where the bathroom is."

"Like this," Pete smiled, signing it for me, and then again at a slower speed. I copied his movements until I got it right and he nodded, "There you go, now you know everything you need," he said, I laughed.

"Part of me really wants to show Hope, and tell her I'm learning, but at the same time, I feel like I don't know enough yet and I need to wait."

"Babies don't wait to talk in full sentences before they start talking, you didn't wait to be MVP before you played in a soccer game," he said.

"My point is, you don't have to know a lot about something before you can start using it, or talking about it. Just like anything else that's new, it'll take time, but you'll get there. Hope knows you're not an expert, but she is, and communicating with her, is probably the quickest way to learn. Think about it this way," he continued, "You know a heck of a lot more then she thinks you do."

"Well I can't argue that," I laughed.

"Hey, it's almost to the hour," Pete looked at his watch, "Help me start setting up?"

"Let's do it," I said as we both stood to leave.

"I think the story's pretty incredible by the way, your brother. You're doing a good thing."

"I hope so," he said, "He deserves it."

*　　*　　*

It was about mid-way through practice and Hope was doing really well. She had run through each drill perfectly; her moves were getting faster and she was ready to score going into the team scrimmage. She made it up the field, and kicked the ball right between the defenders, and into the top corner of the goal. The other volunteers and I all applauded, offering praises to various players, but when Hope ran by, she merely flashed a smile and I gave her a thumbs up in return.

It wasn't long after that, that the scrimmage was over, and practice was coming to a close. Hope and I walked to the side of the field, as other kids did cool-down passes amongst each other. She crouched down by the tree to pick up her water and take a long sip in the afternoon heat. She noticed that I was looking at her and gave me a confused look, probably thinking that I had something to say, and I did. The problem was remembering how to say it.

I decided to go for it, and gave what I remembered to be the sign for "good job", I must have done alright because a look of shock flashed across her face. A little more confidently I signed: "I am taking a class to learn how to sign", something

I had made a point of going over with my teacher enough times so I could get it right. Even if I couldn't sign well, at least she would have an idea of where the signals were coming from.

After that, I stood, unsure of what to do, as she looked at me. I shuffled in my feet, nervously wondering if somehow I had offended her. But a moment later, she broke into a smile and rushed in for a hug. I was both caught off guard, and overtly relieved, at her reaction. When she pulled away, I saw her eyes were watery, and she offered the sign for "thank you". But she didn't need to, her face said everything, and that alone was worth it.

20

At practice the next day, Terry was entirely back to normal. Coaching as feverishly as ever, demanding of our level of play, and giving attitude when she felt necessary, but no more towards me than anyone else. My teammates acted the same too, as though they hadn't witnessed what happened at Saturday's game; everyone seemed to ignore it, including Liv.

I kept expecting Terry to pull me to the side, and talk through our disagreement with me, but she never did. No acknowledgement at all, it was as though it never happened, at least in her mind. But for me, I didn't forget any of it. I did something that made her mad, and she acted like an entirely different person, a mean person, and then later, when she's done being made, she's goes right back to the way things were before, without a word. I wasn't sure I liked that.

Even as practice ended, she merely waved me off like everyone else, got in her car and drove away. Part frustrated, and part confused, I unlocked my bike and swung my leg over, ready to ride off. Liv caught up to me, and jumped on her bike faster than I had ever seen her.

"You weren't gonna ride off without me, were you?" she smiled like the answer was an obvious no. I wanted to say *well you had no problem riding off without me after the game,* but I didn't. I stayed quiet and rode next to her in silence. Pedaling with more ease than I used to, Liv kept looking back at me, having to slow down to match my pace.

"What's wrong with you tonight?" she said as more of a statement than question.

"What do you mean?" I asked.

"You barely coached, or even *talked* at practice, you went to the bikes without me, and now you're falling behind, biking like you've got nowhere in the world to be. What gives?"

"What's the rush?" I wondered.

"Um, we always rush," Liv said as though she couldn't believe I'd ask that. "How else do we have time to practice more in the field, before you have to meet your mom for dinner. Like always."

There was that word again, *always.* I feel like I have a lot of that word in my life, which is fine, if that's what you want. But not everything has to be that way, and you should be able to change your always. Just because you don't want big change, doesn't mean you can't like little ones.

"I don't think it *always* has to be that way," I said softly, "I don't feel like it is anymore anyways."

"What do you mean?" Liv asked with genuine confusion.

"Look, I know that soccer has always been a bond for us and that's awesome," I said. "But we used to hang out just to hang out, and we used to talk about other things too. Now it feels like all you want to do is this team, and be the best friend MVP's, not just the best friends. You do everything Terry says, even when you know it's wrong. The way she was acting towards me at the game, you didn't even flinch. You didn't say anything to her, or even me. In fact, you didn't talk to me at all until she was good with me again today. I love playing soccer, but I'm also finding that I love coaching it at VIP. Which is super cool, and I want to talk to you about it, but I feel like I can't," my eyes went downcast.

I waited a few minutes for Liv to respond, but when she didn't, I took a deep breath and put my right foot back on its pedal.

"I'm gonna head home," I told her, "I'll see you in class tomorrow."

I got on, and rode away, looking back to see her still standing there, arms crossed. A tear rolled down my cheek. Liv and I had never fought about anything, we'd always been so close, but suddenly, I felt so far from her. I meant everything I had said, so I don't think I regret it, but I can't shake the feeling of loss, as though I had just ruined one of the best things in my life. And I missed it already.

21

The next few days in school, Liv took ignoring me to a whole new level. She wouldn't even look in my direction; it's like we never knew each other at all. I thought honesty was supposed to make people closer, but it seemed as though all it did was drive her further away. I started questioning all the possibilities, wondering if there was something I said that came off harsher than planned; but before I could come to any conclusions, it would be time to go to the next class.

Practice was the same, she stood next to me to receive captainship instructions from Terry and that was it, she would perform whatever task alongside me, but without a word. I could tell our teammates noticed the difference. There were murmurs of concern and confusion. They had known Liv and I for years and only known us to be the golden girls of friendship. As much as it already hurt to be a part of it, having all your peers wondering what's wrong, when you don't even know yourself, makes it that much worse.

When I told my mom what happened, she thought that Liv and I should take a few days to separate and think about what was said, and when's it's time for another conversation, we'll know. She encouraged me to go let off some steam, and do something to take my mind off things. It was Wednesday afternoon when she said that, so I knew what I was doing Thursday.

*　　*　　*

Biking back to Ginnen Park, I was even more excited than the first time. The air was cool and the breeze was just soft enough to bat off the afternoon sun. Our Thursday practice time shifted so now the two practices ran back to back. If I leave immediately after and bike really hard, I should only be about ten minutes late to practice with my team. My mom wrote a doctor's note just in case Terry got mad; she agreed I didn't need that right now.

As soon as I dropped my bike, Tadd was over to great me. He ran a hand through his shaggy hair and gave a sideways smile, clearly excited about something.

"What is it?" I asked, starting to feel the excitement for something I didn't even know about.

"Oh, we just got a new player for today," he grinned; I almost laughed.

"I mean okay that's cool but the way you were acting, I thought-" before I could finish, Tadd stepped to the side and revealed the reason he'd rushed up to me before I could look around. Behind him, Hope was there, smiling and bouncing excitedly, dressed head-to-toe in soccer gear.

"Hope?" I gasped, "Are you playing?" In the moment I completely forgot to sign but Hope seemed to get the jist from my surprise as she nodded proudly.

"Of course she is!" Tadd exclaimed. "Haven't you seen this girl play? She's as good as any of us, and I thought you two would make a great team."

"Thank you," I said softly, pulling into him for a hug.

As soon as the game started, Hope and I were perfectly diagonal with each other; her just slightly ahead of me across the field, ready to take the ball forward as soon as I passed it. A defender rushed up on me and I swung my leg back, preparing for the cross. I wanted to yell out to Hope, just to be sure she saw it coming, when it hit me that I couldn't, we hadn't practiced plays or talked through strategy, and now here we were, and once again, we couldn't communicate. Being able to communicate well with teammates while on the field is one of the most coveted skills you could have. A skill that I felt, in that moment, I had lost.

As I hesitated and pondered what to do, the defender took advantage of my lapse in judgement and stole the ball. My fellow forwards and midfielders, including Hope, seemed caught off guard by the change in pace and they all seemed to stop, and look at me for a second, before continuing play. I never lost a ball like that, so easily, without a fight. I shook it off and chased back to the halfway line, waiting for another opportunity. Hope was adjacent to me, across the line, watching curiously as the midfielders battled a dozen yards away.

I stirred the dirt with my toe, wondering how to effectively combat my newfound difficulty. Then I remembered, when I had Pete as a coach, he had a system, a numbering system. A lot of coaches do it, where you number out your fingers and they mean different plays, but with Pete, it was even more divided. Different numbers were like phrases, 1 "pass forward", 2 "I'm running", 3 "pass back", 4 "my ball" and so on. All you had to do was hold the right number of fingers in the air for the whole team to see, and no one else would pick up on it because they were expecting an elaborate play. I began to ponder if Pete had made that system from his interest in signing and non-verbal communication. When I thought back on memories of that team, everything seemed connected.

I gazed to the side until I was able to catch Hope's eye and wave her over. She hesitated as the ball wasn't too far from us, but jogged over, keeping one eye on our backline. I knew we were short on time but this system just might work. We signed back and forth for a couple minutes and the ball crawled closer, just seconds before we were back in the game, we looked at each other and smiled, we were gonna try.

The ball shot over the halfway line and Hope darted back to her side to retrieve it, just barely reaching it before the other team's defensive line, she held two fingers in the air and charged up line. The rest of the team was confused but I knew what she meant. I chased after her, pulling into the center just slightly, but keeping my body open to the other team's goal, prepared to run with it at any time. Two defenders came up on her and she rolled the ball back, throwing three fingers up. I paced back a few steps as she twisted her body and sent the ball right to my feet. The other team's back midfielder pounced in front of me and I tapped the ball through their legs, grabbing it from the other side and pulling towards the center. It was me and the last defender. The others were coming towards me from the sides, all the focus was on me. Hope lingered to the right of the goal, watching me, she was just far enough to the side that the other team didn't see her as an immediate threat, so I knew to make her one. I put one finger up and chipped the ball over the defender's heads, landing it perfectly between Hope and the goal. She ran toward it as a midfielder sprinted back and leaped at the ball. Hope hit it with the inside of her foot, so tight on time that she ended up sliding on the ground immediately after kicking it.

It felt like slow-motion watching the ball roll into the lower corner of the goal. The pace just fast enough for the keeper to fall a second behind and miss it. 1 - 0. I screamed and ran towards Hope, tackling her to the ground in excitement. I couldn't believe it. She had been told her whole life that she couldn't play with "normal kids", and first quarter of her first game with those "normal kids", she's the first person to change the scoreboard. So, what are they saying about normal? Nobody has the same talent, we all have different ones, so what does skill have to do with it? We had a love for the same game, and we play better together, I'd say that makes us equal.

22

After the final whistle blew, Hope and I went to the side of the field with Tadd and Keller. They asked me to sign to her that they were proud, and when I did it correctly, I beamed with a little pride myself. We chatted for a few minutes before they walked off to join Jane, Louis and a couple others, leaving Hope and I to talk about the game a little longer.

We signed back and forth for a while before I began looking about the field. I saw a young bunny hop out from behind a bush, slowly but surely, across the field, I outstretched my arm to point it out to Hope when my watch caught my eye.

"Oh no, is that the time?!" I said, having completely forgotten about my practice. Hope looked at me with confusion. I tapped the face of my watch anxiously and signed "I'm sorry" to her before sprinting to my bike and pedaling off as fast as I could.

By the time I reached my own team, I was almost a half hour late. Feeling immensely grateful for my fake doctor's note, I quickly handed it to Terry and she scrunched up her nose, but said nothing. I immediately got into line along with the rest of my team and worked extra hard through the rest of practice, despite the fact I'd been tired before I had even arrived for it.

Throughout the night, I caught Liv looking at me a couple of times, but never in the eye, and never for more than a few seconds. I wanted so badly to talk to her, about the fight, about the team, about school, anything, I just missed my best friend.

At the end of practice, Terry came up to me, and I prepared myself for the criticism I was undoubtedly about to receive. But when she stopped in front of me, she almost looked happy.

"Nadia, you looked good today, when your peers were struggling, you stepped in to help, without compromising your own performance. That's what I've been looking for," she said, clipboard in one hand, with the other clutching her hip. "Despite some mishaps and misjudgments," she looked at me with clear accusation. "You really do lead this team, I look forward to seeing more of that as the tournament nears. But until then," she gave me a sharp look," I don't want any other appointment conflicts. I expect you to be here at each and every practice. Understood?"

I gave her the smug hint of a smile before she walked away. I wasn't sure how to feel, happy that she finally complimented me? Or upset that she still held blame over my head? As I turned to go, I looked at the racks, hoping to see Liv waiting, but as I assumed, her bike was already gone.

23

After the next VIP, Hope and I
sat in the grass and talked for a while.
I told her why I had to leave so
quickly, and explained, as best I
could, what was going on with Liv. I
still only knew simple signs, so it was
hard for me to tell if she understood
as she watched my hands and
remained silent. It was only after I
was done that she responded, saying
that she was sorry, and hoped it
would get better.

The sound of an engine
shutting off came from the lot, we
turned to see Hope's mom stepping
out of her silver mini-van and making
her way towards us. Hope and I stood
together and took a few steps
forward to meet her. I reintroduced
myself in sign and her mom smiled in

a mix of surprise and appreciation. Hope turned to give me a quick hug and wave good-bye, but before they left, I signed to her, asking if she wanted to hang out sometime, outside of VIP. Hope looked taken aback for a minute before bursting into a smile and nodding excitedly. I smiled back and she gave me her phone number so that I could text her later to plan a time.

Going back home that night, I felt peaceful, Sundays had become so relaxed compared to the rest of the week. As I put my bike away, I walked in to find my mom scribbling words down on a little notepad.

"What's that?" I asked.

"Grocery list, what else?" she smiled, "Come with me to the store?"

"Sure," I almost laughed, "Just let me change."

*   *   *

I rolled a tomato over in my hand and felt for texture.

"This one's good," I handed it to my mom.

"Nice and soft, perfect for risotto," she said, placing it in the cart, "Go pick out an avocado while I get zucchini and then we'll be done."

"Okay," I said, walking around to the other side of the organic's section. I stuck my hand in the bin and pulled out a plump avocado. When no one was looking, I ticked off the notch at the top of the fruit, revealing a tiny crater in a bright green color. I smirked, perfectly ripe, and turned to bring it back to my mom. But as I moved to the side, I bumped into someone else's cart.

"Sorry!" they said from a crouched position behind the cart, attempting to retrieve a salad bag.

"Oh, hi Colleen," my mom said, walking up from behind me as the lady stood to face us. I bit my lip, Liv's mom.

"Inna, Nadia, hi," she said with some mild discomfort.

"Hi," I said back, shuffling my feet.

"Well, how are you both?" she asked with a raised brow. As my mom responded, I couldn't help but notice how much she resembled Liv, they could be twins.

"Nadia," my mom nudged me.

"What? Sorry, spaced out for a second," I said.

"I was just asking how VIP was," she said, "Liv told me about it."

"It's great!" I said. "It's a great program and it's really cool cause even though I'm technically in the teaching position, I've learned a lot from the other kids, and everyone's super nice there too."

"Well between coaching that and coaching your own team, you must be running yourself dry," Colleen commented. I forced a slight laugh and smile, but I couldn't help but feel she hadn't meant it in the friendliest way.

We continued the awkward pleasantries for a few minutes until we were given an escape route when someone else Colleen knew came by and they started to chat. I quickly waved good-bye and we made for the checkout. As the clerk ran each item through the scanner, I took it and began bagging. I looked over and saw Colleen, still talking to the other person, her smile and expression much more genuine with them. I know I had talked to my mom about what happened with Liv, but only cause I wanted to talk, not because I wanted to get her on my side. In fact, my mom didn't take a side at all, she listened with empathy and offered advice. I hadn't seen either of us as "the bad guy", but I couldn't help but feel like Liv had made me out to be.

24

I felt like my head was spinning all day long. School until 3 pm, soccer until 5, class till 6:30, and now here, almost seven at night, and I was finally getting home. But my day wasn't over yet. I heard a knock on the door and rushed across the house to answer it. I opened it to find a smiling Hope, holding a soccer ball up on her hip. *Homework can wait*, I thought.

"Mom, we're going to the park!" I called.

"Be back in a half hour for dinner," she reminded me.

Hope and I looked at each other and smiled, dashing down the steps and across the greenbelt. We played for almost 40 minutes, weaving in and out of trees, playing 1v1 and practicing shooting between the berry bushes until my mom came out of the house, arms crossed, looking at me. I fluttered my eyes at her glare,

"Has it been a half hour?" I asked innocently; she rolled her eyes and asked if Hope would like to stay for dinner. I turned and asked her through sign and she nodded.

After dinner, I started rummaging through our pantry, in the mood for something sweet. I pulled out a brownie mix and held it up for Hope to see from the other side of the counter. She nodded and I grabbed the mixing bowl.

The strong scent of chocolate wafted through the kitchen as Hope and I cracked eggs against the side of the bowl. The yokes seeped through, along with plenty of eggshell; we laughed as we used a fork to spar them apart. Once the mix was stirred into silk, I dumped in a packet of rainbow sprinkles for good measure. Hope opened the oven and I slid the tray in and set the timer before she moved to close it back up.

We waited and watched our creation come to life from behind the oven's glass door. The scent grew stronger and richer as we struggled to wait it out until it was done. The minutes ticked on, until at last, I watched the 60-second countdown begin. Then 30 seconds, and then ten, the longest of them all. Finally, the timer dinged, and we bolted to the door, throwing on oven mitts and pulling out the tray. As soon as it was on the counter, it was free game, we were tired of waiting. We dug into the brownie pan and let the warm chocolate melt in our mouths, not even caring as it burned our throats.

25

Sweat streaked down my dirt-clad legs as I pulled myself up from the ground after a fall. The sun beat down aggressively, and the team was feeling the heat. We were all exhausted, today's game had hit us harder than usual. The whole team felt disorganized and out-of-whack. Liv and I weren't talking, our teammates were practically trying to steal the ball from each other, and we lost to a team that we usually beat handedly, which didn't set us up well for the pending tournament. The brackets were starting next weekend and I wasn't feeling confident.

As the whistle blew, Terry called us in and I prepared myself for the fire. Her face said it all: anger, disappointment, confusion, frustration, you name it, and all with pursed lips and tightly wrapped knuckles.

"As you all know, this is a team that you have triumphed over for the past three years without a hinge of doubt. Now, would anyone like to tell me what happened?" she moved hands to the cuts of her hips and looked down on us, taking great advantage of our middle school height. After a few moments of silence, Jenna raised a shaky arm. Terry looked at her in a challenging way, waiting to see if her confidence would waver, but she kept her arm up, and I applauded her for that.

"I think the field was pretty quiet," she started. "We weren't communicating the way we usually do. I feel like we didn't really know where each other were on the field, and we weren't giving advice or anything during plays. I guess I just mean, we weren't playing to help each other," she stuttered. "I'm not sure why, just an observation."

Terry looked at her for a minute, as did the rest of us, before responding. *We weren't playing to help each other,* I replayed her words in my mind. I agreed with her as she said it, but I hadn't thought about it like that before. I wondered when that started, and why I never noticed. Although I guess that's exactly it, I never noticed, because I was thinking about my own play, not our team's. Maybe that was the whole problem.

"I see your observation Jenna," Terry started, "It is true that communication is a vital thing that it appears we lost. But like you said, it was just an observation, and observations aren't helpful right now. I need solutions, fixes to the obvious problems. Anyone who can help with that?" She looked out at us and Jenna curved in on herself. I felt bad for her, she was just trying to help, but once again, Terry seemed to be letting out a cruel side that none of us knew.

"Well, if no one is going to provide helpful discussion points, then we're done discussing. But it is your effort that you put into the game, both emotionally and physically, that will decide the outcome of your play. We received the rest of the tournament schedule this morning. Next week, as you know, we start brackets. The following week, our placement will determine where we are for tournament games. And the week after, the final games. Clear your schedule for all three weekends, conflicts are not an option, especially that last weekend. Mark your calendars because that Sunday, April 14, is the date of the consolation and championship games. If you can get it together, and play like you should, we should have no problem getting there. But that's up to you, you have to want it. You may have Friday off, but that's it, the rest of the week, practice every day, two hours a day. Be there, if you want to be a part of this tournament. But don't waste my time if you're not going to step up and play real soccer."

And with that, she walked off, away from the field, across the parking, into her car, and down the street, without a look, a good-bye, a gesture, nothing. We all stood there without her for a few minutes before leaving. Not talking, just looking at each other, wondering if we really did want it. The way the last few weeks had gone, I wasn't so sure. It wasn't just me anymore, everyone was frustrated, frustrated with Terry, with the game, with each other. She told us to step up and play real soccer but she was the one keeping us from just that. Practicing drill after drill, and play after play, leaving everything to strategy and nothing to instinct. Taking out the fun.

26

Maybe Terry didn't give us quite the pep talk that she thought. The next few practices ran about as smoothly as the game, bumping into each other, forgetting plays, not caring when things went wrong, or even on the occasion they went right. The only fun I had all week was at the pick-up game, running around with Hope, Tadd, Keller, and others who truly loved the game. The only way I could fit it in, was to take an earlier sign class, go straight to the park, leave 15 minutes early to make sure I got to practice on time, and rush through homework sometime between dinner and bed.

But today was Friday, and I had never been so excited to not have practice. I even choose to skip a day of ASL class in order to have the whole afternoon to just have fun. After school, I went home and changed out of my jeans and into pajamas, even throwing on a sweater that was two-sizes too big. I had headphones on as I lay in my bed, when my mom came through the door. I pulled the earbuds out and sat up straight against my pillow.

"Is that how you dress for company?" she asked with a slight laugh. She moved out of the way and revealed Hope behind her. She waved and I smiled back, inviting her to sit next to me. I caught her up on my hectic week and she told me about hers with a special surprise, her family was going to adopt a puppy, one she could train to help her communicate her needs. I smiled at the good news, knowing how isolated Hope felt sometimes, I'm sure a new friend would be the best thing for her.

*   *   *

I reached across the floor to pull out a couple more beads from the plastic bin to Hope's right. Metallic blue, purple and silver, decorated in an Ombre effect across their strand, surrounding four white block letters spelling out "HOPE", just like the one I had for Lesya. And for me, Hope used gold, burgundy, and shiny rust-colored beads, all organized in a perfect pattern of twos, encircling the word "Nadia". I flipped over the bracelet, added two smaller beads and tied it together on the ends. I smiled as I slipped it on my wrist, and shook it in front of Hope's face to show it off. She applauded before finishing her own and petting her wrist dramatically. We both erupted in laughter until we were cut off by my mom opening my door.

"Sorry to interrupt," she said, "But your sisters' on the phone," she held out the receiver, and I stood to take it from her. "And when you're done with that, you better clean up this mess," she said sternly, gazing over the array of crafts we had let loose on my floor. "I'll start making dinner in a half hour," she told me before walking out.

"Hi," I said into the phone, then turning to Hope to sign out the letters L.E.S.Y.A. She nodded and began gathering the loose beads to put back in their bin. "How are you?" I asked, "Getting enough sleep and food? Are they working you too hard?"

"Not really, yes, and I knew what I was signing up for. But yes, big yes on the food," she laughed, "We are surprisingly well fed over here."

"But it's not like mom's," I said.

"Nothing ever is," she agreed. "Although I do remember you baking some pretty fantastic make-your-own pizza's," she said.

"With vegetables, fruit, cheese, beans, the occasional pasta bake on top," I said.

"Whatever you could find." I could tell she was smiling too.

"Anyway," she continued, "How are you doing? How's soccer,

VIP, friends, what's going on? It's been a few weeks."

"Funny you should ask," I sat straighter and motioned for Hope to come over, she looked confused but made her way over to sit next to me. "Can I switch you to skype real fast?" I asked.

"Um, yeah, I just have to go in the other room, give me a second," she said, I could hear her footsteps echoing on cement floors. "Everything okay?"

"Yeah everything's great," I said.

"Okay," she said, "I'm going to switch you over."

Her voice went out and I put down the phone, moving my laptop onto my bed. The screen went black for a second, before her photo pulled up with a request to chat. I clicked on the icon, and suddenly my sister's face was before me. I hadn't seen her in so long.

We looked at each other for a minute and I could see the start of tears beginning to well in her eyes. I wanted to stay right there and keep looking, and talking, and forgetting about everything else, but I knew her call time was limited, and there was something I had to do.

"Lesya, there is someone I want you to meet," I said, turning the screen until she could see both of us, "Lesya, this is Hope."

But before I could continue with the other side of the

introduction, Lesya beat me to it. She signed her own introduction to Hope, and Hope responded back with: "Nice to meet you Lesya."

"You know sign language?!" I asked with a mix of impressment and betrayal.

"Of course I do," she smirked, "English, Russian, Arabic, Spanish, ASL, currently working on Mandarin."

"Show off," I rolled my eyes. "But why didn't you tell me? You could have helped me figure stuff out," I complained.

"It was for you to figure out on your own," she said simply. "Now, what are we talking in English for?"

She turned back to Hope and began asking her questions. I tried to follow along, but between the two of them, I felt even more behind than usual. At first, I was too intimidated to even try and participate, but after watching the flow of their conversation for a few minutes, I got my bearings, and began to respond with simple answers. They both seemed to look at me with pride, and after a while, it all felt natural.

Hope was in the middle of asking Lesya how long it would be before she came home, when an alarm went off from the other side of the call. Lesya watched the flashes before looking back at the camera with sad eyes. I knew what that meant.

"I'm sorry," she said, then signing to Hope that she had to go. A moment later, the screen clicked off and my spirits dropped, I had a feeling it would be awhile before we could talk again.

Hope put her hand on my arm and told me how nice it was to meet her, and that we had the same eyes. I smiled at that. Then thinking back on our conversation, I knew what Lesya would say we should do tonight. I checked the clock and quickly got up from my bed, motioning for Hope to follow me out the door. Just as my mom was pulling out a pot from under the stove, my socks helped me slide across the tile in front of her.

"Hey," I said.

"Hi," she laughed.

"I don't want you to cook," I said.

"Well, that's offensive," she put one hand on her hip.

"I mean, Hope and I want to make dinner tonight," I said. She looked at me for a second, a little off-put, then bent down to put the pan back in its drawer.

"I'll be back in a half hour," she smiled, walking out of the kitchen and down the hall.

As soon as she was gone, I dug into the fridge. I found two cornmeal pizza crusts and slapped them on the counter, bits of ice flying off the edges and onto the ground. I looked up at Hope and she nodded in agreement. Pretty soon, it felt like we were pulling out the entire contents of the fridge. We put the ingredients of the first crust to one side, figs, cherries, and balsamic, our version of gourmet. And for the second, I found a box of mac n'cheese mix and held it out excitedly. At first, Hope looked at me like I was crazy, then she gave it some thought and shrugged, starting a pot of water on the stove. As soon as it reached a low boil, I poured in the mix and began to stir. Sharp cheddar quickly became the aroma of the kitchen.

We scooped out some sample pieces and high-fived at our efforts. Once I'd gotten it all out in the strainer, Hope and I laughed as we placed the macaroni pieces on top of the marinara-covered crust. Topping it off with a few extra shreds of cheese, just in case, we slid the pizzas into the already-warm oven. We shut the door, and the countdown began.

After meandering back into my room, Hope started teaching me some new signs. We created a system where I would point to something, and she would respond with how to sign it. While at the park, she had taught me how to talk about trees, bikes, even the pond. And now here, she signed out expressions for "book", "desk", "computer", and "homework". I told her I didn't need the last one and she laughed. Out of nowhere, I heard my mom scream my name. Hope and I looked at each other, rushed out the door, and into the kitchen. It was hazy and smelled like smoke. My mom waved at the air, opened the oven door and pulled out two very burnt pizzas.

"Did you even set a timer?!" she asked, rushing around the room to open windows and doors. As the smokiness began to fade, I looked down at the pizzas, definitely char-dusted, but they didn't look ruined. I picked off a few pieces of the macaroni, and tossed them in my mouth. Despite the fact that I should have blown on it, before burning my mouth again, it wasn't bad.

"Not my plan," I admitted, "But I actually like it." Hope was trying to suppress a smile; my mom rolled her eyes and used oven mitts to plop our dinner down on the table, forks and all.

"Bon Appetit."

27

My alarm dinged at exactly 7:30; I slapped it off the table with the back of my hand. It flew right into the arms of a giant stuffed bear, emblazoned with the Russian flag. I lifted myself slowly, rubbing my stomach as I sat up, still full from last night's dinner.

I made my way to the kitchen, and plucked a banana from the fruit bowl, my pre-game side-cramp prevention. Once I'd finished it, I tossed the peel into the bushes in my backyard, and went back inside to get my uniform. The air was crisp so I opted for an underlayer, one arm at a time, pulling up the sleeves to my wrists, and linking the little holes over my thumbs. I wrapped an insulated headband over my ears, pulled long socks over my shin guards, threw my cleats in my backpack, and went out the side gate to retrieve my bike.

A few minutes ahead of schedule, I pedaled lightly around the greenbelt, I would be there right on time. The wind kicked up and I hugged a little closer to myself, beginning to pedal faster just for the factor of warmth. Once I arrived, I tied my bike to the tree and jogged to meet my team. Half the girls were yet to arrive, and when I said hi to Terry, she didn't even bother to respond. Everyone was quiet, it felt eerie, and I wasn't sure why.

The silence continued up until the start of the game. As I took my spot at center forward, I felt uncomfortable with the atmosphere.

Something was off, but I didn't know what.

Once the game started, I let go of it all, and played my game. The team did better than last weekend, but they were still playing with too much riding on strategy, and not enough on instinct. It was no secret that I was working twice as hard as the rest of my team, quarter after quarter, but it was because I didn't feel like I was working. I wasn't playing like it was competition, I was playing like it was a game that I loved, and for the first time since we got into the tournament, I really felt that again.

The whistle blew, and I ended the game with a hat trick. Liv had scored one, and the other team two. We were looking good going into the next game. We had an 8 am tomorrow that would be our final qualification for next weekend's tournament style games.

As usual, our team moved to the far side and stood in a circle around Terry as she went over her thoughts on the game. Play by play commentary, and she never offered a single congratulations to me for my three goals. She did however, mention that Liv's goal was: "a beautiful display on what we'd learned in practice." But nothing directed at me. And nothing from my teammates either, none of them had patted my back, or said "good job", I was beginning to feel that eeriness again. Before we all turned to go, Terry stopped us and said she had one more thing.

"As you all know, I spoke with Liv and Nadia about the captainship long before we even knew that we were in the tournament," she started; I watched Liv's face fall. "I explained from the beginning, that it would require a great deal of discipline and commitment. There could be no lack of effort, or leadership, over the team. They were to be examples, a lot of pressure no doubt. Maybe, too much pressure," she said sternly; I braced myself for whatever great blow was about to hit. "Nadia and I have communicated on this in an updated form in the past, and, as of yesterday, she made it clear to me that she no longer wants this responsibility." I looked up and stared her dead in the eye. "And therefore," she continued without a beat, "Nadia will no longer be a captain alongside Liv. Jenna," she called, Jenna averted my eyes and moved to stand next to Terry, "We talked about this last night, and I would like to officially say it in front of your teammates. Jenna will be your new co-captain. Any questions on the game, or information about the team, from here on out, please go to one of them."

My jaw practically hit the floor. I had seen the other side of Terry, but I never expected this. My teammates glanced uncomfortably at me, trying to see if, this was in fact, a mutual decision. Liv looked at the ground, shaking her head ever so slightly. I could pretend I was part of the decision and make everything easy. I could, but I won't.

"Excuse me?" I said. Terry looked up, as though surprised I had decided to say something. "What exactly do you mean by my making it clear to you yesterday, when I didn't even see you, that I know longer want the responsibility?" I asked, crossing my arms, and with all the attitude I desired.

"Exactly that," she said. "You didn't see me yesterday, because you didn't show up to practice, therefore, openly showing your lack of commitment for us all to see."

"You told us there was no Friday practice," I said, not caring that we had the entire team for an audience.

"And then I changed my mind, just like you did about your team," she said. "I sent out an email saying practice was back on."

"When?"

"Yesterday at three, two hours' notice to the change in schedule," she said, crossing her arms back at me.

"I only check my email once a day in the mornings. Two hours isn't a warning, it's asking us to be on stand-by," I said, a little proud of my sassy confidence.

"It was enough for everyone else," she said, motioning to the team. They all ducked their heads and avoided eye contact. "And, even if it was an accident, it wasn't the first time, you've skipped a practice before, and let's not forget the time you were late with a fake doctor's note."

"I made a fake doctor's note because you treat me like this whenever I make a mistake. I'm tired of feeling like I'm not enough no matter how hard I try. And I'm tired of dreading the practices for a game that I love. I'm sorry that I didn't see your email, but I didn't see your email. I didn't skip practice, I didn't know we had one. But even if I did, how is it okay for you to take away a position you gave me, and tell the whole team your decision, without even telling me?" I asked, completely over my own embarrassment, and knowing I deserved better; Liv looked up at me for the first time.

"Regardless of what your coaching methods are, and how I feel about them, you're still my coach. And I still respect you," I said, ready to walk away, but pausing for a second and turning back around. "But I'm still your player, one of your twelve players, that play the game you coach. So, maybe you should respect us a little too."

With that, I strode away, not even shedding a tear, because for once, I didn't question whether I was right. I knew I was. Once I was to my bike, I heard footsteps running after me but I didn't turn around.

"Nadia!" a voice called. It was Liv. I stopped short, my fingers tightly wrapped over the right handlebar.

"Nadia wait," she said; I turned to face her. "I'll go talk to Terry, if you're not a captain, then I shouldn't be either."

"Liv, I would never ask you to give up being a captain. I don't want you to, you're great at it, and you deserve the position. I appreciate the offer but you don't have to do that, really. And besides, I'm sure half the reason she took me off, is because she sees we don't communicate anymore," I admitted, with immediate regret.

"I know I don't have to, I'm offering," she said with a little edge. "I'll drop being a captain for you, because you're my best friend, and because that's what you do for your friends, but I'm still angry! It's not my fault we're not in sync like we used to be. You're prioritizing VIP and Hope over your own team, over me!"

"Liv it's not like that," I
promised.

"Then what is it?" she asked, a
tear rolling down her cheek, "You
haven't been the same towards me
ever since you started going to VIP. I
feel like you don't even want to be
around me, and like everything I do is
wrong." She started crying and my
eyes began to water, I felt a pang in
my stomach. "Why don't you want to
be my friend anymore?" she asked
with pleading eyes: "I miss you."

"I miss you too," I said, moving
forward to wrap her in a hug. I was
half-expecting her to protest, and she
hesitated as it crossed her mind, but
she gave in, and her tears ran down
my shoulder.

"I don't want to be different, and I don't want us to be different. I love our team, but I don't like the way Terry is coaching it. Coaches should encourage and motivate you, but ever since we got into the tournament, I feel like she's made me resentful towards soccer. And probably towards you too," I said sadly. "But I don't want to be, it's not your fault. I have new things I like, that doesn't make me a new person. And I want to share them with you!" I said, grabbing her hand. "Come with me to a pick-up game, you'll love it, it's just a bunch of people who love soccer." I looked at the ground, "It's kind of nice to just play for fun and because I love the game, not just play to win. And VIP! You can meet Hope and see what it's all about. Your dad won't mind if you miss a couple hours on one Sunday, please, just try it, I want you to go with me," I pleaded. She looked to the ground for a few minutes, I could see her contemplating it in her mind, but then she looked up at me with the hint of a smile, and I knew.

"Okay," she said, "I'll try it."

28

The next morning, the game went as well as the day before. I didn't say a word to Terry, or my teammates, about the captainship, and I was going to keep it that way. I had said what I needed to say. I wasn't going to let it prevent me from enjoying the tournament, and I wasn't going to let it keep me from playing. In fact, without the pressure of her watching eye and constant criticism, I actually had more fun at the game than I had in weeks. Liv and I both scored two, and we came out of the game leading the other team by a point, which kept us in good position for next weekend. The rest of our team, however, was still running disorganized, and the communication on the field was just as limited as before. It was no longer my role as a captain to change it, but I still felt it was my role as a teammate, I just needed to figure out how.

After the game, Liv biked back to my house with me. We sat at the counter and ate store-bought sandwiches while slurping down glasses of chocolate milk. Nothing tastes better after a game.

Leaving a good half hour earlier than normal, we got back on our bikes, and went across town the other direction, to where they held VIP. I had called Pete last night, asking if he could meet us there to give Liv a rundown on the Buddy training.

We biked in silence, not in the same way we had before, it wasn't angry silence, it was more that we just didn't know what to say. For weeks now, we had been pitted against each other, the bitterness had been lying in wait until it finally came out, but now that it did, and we made up, it was hard to pretend like it didn't happen. Every few minutes, one of us would say something to the other, ask a question or make a joke, and it was fine, but it still felt forced. It was like we were walking on eggshells, trying to be overly nice to make up for the times we were mean, but that's not what friendship is. We weren't mad, but we weren't normal, the tension was still there.

Pete was ready to go as soon as we got there, PowerPoint and all. He went over the slides, bullet points and examples, without missing a beat. Every now and then, he would check in with Liv to see how she was doing and then look to me to offer advice or talk about specific situations I had dealt with on the field. It was clear that Liv was overwhelmed, she was looking at each slide and listening hard, she was trying, but it was a lot, and despite our continued awkwardness, I felt lucky to not only have her here with me, but as a friend at all.

The slideshow finished just in time, and he went to get Liv a shirt from the back. I turned to her as soon as he left the room, and rested my chin over the crook of my elbow.

"What do you think?" I asked.

"I don't know Nadia," she wavered. "I know I said I would try, but this is a lot of information, and I feel like I don't know enough. I mean, I've never done anything like this, ever," she said nervously, rubbing her palms together.

"Sure you have!" I said. "You're a team captain, and you're great at it, you know how to coach, you know how to lead, and you get that people have different strengths, that's all you need."

She couldn't hide her expression when I said captain, she was clearly shocked that I brought it up. I was a little surprised myself. But after saying it, I realized that I didn't care. I cared that Terry told the team before me, I cared that she told Jenna before me. I care about my team, and

I care about soccer, but I don't need a title in order for people to see that. If I had known that hanging out with Hope that night would have resulted like it did, I still would have done it, it was the best night I'd had in weeks. I felt more self-worth spending time with one good friend, than I did having a group of sort-of friends listen to me. I didn't need to be a captain, I just needed to be me.

After Liv got her shirt on, she followed me back out the building, and over to the field. It was only a few minutes wait, and an introduction to Keller, before I saw Hope walking up the hill. I smiled and waved, she perked up when she saw me and ran down the close side to where I was. We met in a hug, but she pulled back when she saw Liv, confused. I introduced them, and she nodded her head, as though she was in on a secret. As we began walking away, ball between my feet, Hope commented to me that we looked tired. I told her about our game this morning and she nodded accordingly. It was when I looked over at Liv, that I realized she had been left out. Moving away from the group, and into the shade, I plopped the ball down and passed it to Liv.

"You two start passing," I said. "I have to ask Pete something, I'll be back in a minute." Liv looked at me in a panic. "Don't worry," I assured her, "She doesn't bite, just pass it around, I'll be right back."

"Everything okay?" Pete asked, once I had reached him back at the registration desk.

"Yeah," I said, "I told them I needed to ask you something."

"And?" he wondered.

"I don't," I clarified; he laughed. "Just wanted to let them get a feel for each other."

"Ah, not a bad idea," he said. "Well, while you're here, if you want to take a few minutes to go over these game papers for me, and make sure our numbers all match-up, that would be great," he handed me a white packet.

"Game papers?" I asked, looking over the first sheet.

"Yep, the end of season VIP game," he said. "We stop for the summer starting a few weeks from today and – wait, don't you remember talking about this at the beginning of the season?" he asked; I raised a brow with no recognition. "Oh," he said, "We went over it at that practice you missed, a week or two into you first coming I think."

"Oh," I said, looking at the ground. "That practice," I stirred the dirt with the toe of my cleat. "Well what is it?"

"We practice ten-week seasons in the fall and spring, you joined partway through the spring season, which means we're about to end for summer. In order for the kids to have something at the end to look forward to, I always try to pull together a game with a local team, one that runs a similar program to us. I found one a couple towns away, and it looks like we're good to do it on the 14th," he smiled.

"The 14th," I said, feeling a weight grow in my chest, "The 14th of this month?!"

"Yep!" he said, "I'm going to tell the kids at the end of practice today, they're going to be so excited! Especially Hope, it'll be her first game with a team like this. Her mom told me that she did a similar program before, but the other kids had been playing for years and didn't want her to play with them because she wasn't as good, so she quit early. Her mom practically had to force her to try a few days with us. But I don't think it was our program that kept her here," he said with a glint in his eye, "It was you. You brought her confidence back, I mean now look at her," he pointed across the field, "That's all you."

I followed his finger to where Liv and Hope had been joined by a few others in their game. It was clear that Hope was running the show, pointing and putting out cones, pulling out a drill we'd done together a few weeks ago. The others joined in gleefully. Even Liv was smiling; a little more relaxed, watching Hope, and meeting the other kids. I kept looking from one face to the other. *No, I* thought, *It's all her.*

*   *   *

"So, what are you gonna do?" Liv asked once we were a couple blocks from my house. Just like he had said, Pete made the big game announcement at the end of practice.

The kids all cheered, but no one had smiled as big as Hope. She kept looking at me, and then back at her teammates, clapping her hands and beaming with excitement. She had glanced back at me and signed: *I'll show you what I can do.*

"Do about what?" I asked innocently.

"The game," she said. "I know you and Hope have gotten close, and we both know our game is gonna conflict with hers. She's expecting you to go, you need to tell her you can't, she deserves to hear it from you."

"I don't want to think about it right now," I said, stopping my bike. "I want," I paused, "I want to play, play like we used to." I swung my leg over the bike, clicked on the brake, and pulled a ball from the net on my bag. "You in?" I asked; she smiled, snatching the ball from my hands.

"Only if you're in to lose," she smirked, dropping it to the ground and dribbling off at high speed.

"You're on!" I said, chasing after her. Running through the greenbelt, the late afternoon sun, practicing made-up moves; for the first time in weeks, I really felt like I had Liv back.

29

"I'm glad I went, really," Liv said. "And you were right, as soon as I told my dad what it was, he was totally cool with me going."

"I'm glad," I said, "It was so great to have you there, and have you meet Hope!"

"She's a good player," Liv said.

"I know, and you should see her in the pick-up games," I said. "Hey, why don't you?"

"Why don't I what?" Liv raised a brow, leaning over the back of her chair and onto my desk.

"Come to a pick-up game! I told you before that I wanted you to, please, you would have so much fun!" I pleaded.

"Nadia, I know you want me to go to one, and I know you don't like the way Terry coaches, and I'm right there with you, but honestly I'm not like you. You're upset for an afternoon, and then you're over it. You don't mind being at odds with people if it's what you believe in. But I do mind. I would love to play like that again, but Terry's not just gonna change without a fight, and I'm not the person to stand on my own and fight," Liv admitted, shrugging her shoulders and moving to turn back towards the front of the classroom.

"What if you didn't have to stand on your own?" I said quickly. "What if the whole team stood with you?" I smirked at her questioning gaze: "I have an idea."

30

Dear Team,

There's been a change in venue for our next practice. We will be participating in the Thursday night pick-up game held at Ginnen Park at 7pm. Get there a little early for warm-up stretches. This will replace our regular Thursday practice. Get ready to play some real soccer. See you there!

Your Team Captains,

Jenna and Liv

I was between Liv and Jenna on my living room sofa, squished together against the soft pillows. I handed them each the laptop individually to type their names on the bottom of the email I'd written.

Jenna signed immediately and handed it back to me, I passed it along to Liv and she took a deep breath as she clicked each of the three letters.

"Are you sure this is a good idea?" Liv asked, "I'm worried."

"I told you I'd send my own email explaining the whole thing if you want," I offered. "It just has a little more power coming from you guys, since I'm not a captain anymore."

"I'm sorry, again," Jenna bit her lip. "I didn't want to take anything from you, Terry just presented as though you'd quit."

"It's fine, really," I said. "I don't need to be a captain. But I do need to bring our team to one of these games, I really think it'll help."

"But Terry's gonna be so mad," Liv shuffled nervously. "I guess that's the point, right?"

"This isn't about getting back at Terry, well, maybe a little bit," I admitted. "I want her to hear our voices yes, but what this is really about, is getting the team back to where we should be. If Terry gets mad, she gets mad, she can't kick us all off the team. Besides, once she sees how much better we'll play, how can she be mad?" I readied the email to click send.

"How can you be so sure?" Liv asked.

"It worked for me," I said. "It made me remember how much I love soccer, and how good it feels to be around other people who feel the same. This is about teamwork. In order to play like a team, you have to practice like a team, and we haven't been," I said; neither of them could deny that. "You guys in?" I asked, looking from one face to the other.

"I'm in," Jenna said confidently. "I trust you."

We both looked at Liv; she worked her jaw as she re-read the email for the tenth time. She took another deep breath and looked up at us with a smile.

"Send it."

31

It was 6:45, and my teammates were beginning to arrive. One by one, from bikes, cars, even one walking in from the adjoining neighborhood. Liv, Jenna, and I stood by the path, ready to greet them and explain how everything was gonna work. A few of them questioned if Terry was there, another group had already assumed she wouldn't be, but when we told them the truth, there wasn't a single girl who wanted to leave before playing.

Tadd walked over and caught me by the elbow.

"Hey!" I said, giving him a hug. "I didn't know if you'd be here, you weren't at VIP."

"Visiting my brother," he said. "I see that you brought a bit of crowd with you tonight," he looked over the growing group of girls.

"Uh yeah, so Tadd, this is my team," I said, splaying out my arms, "Girls, this is Tadd," they all waved. "You already met Keller, and you'll be meeting Louis and Jane in a minute, actually, I'll go grab them now."

Tadd walked off with me; we made our way across the park to where the other group had gathered. He branched off from me to join some other friends, as I walked up to Jane.

"Keller already told us," she said before I could. "We think it's great, in fact," she looked to Louis for reassurance, "We want to play, team versus team, you guys against us."

"One condition," I said, putting up a finger and pointing forward to the bright-eyed girl walking toward me. "We get Hope." She smiled at everyone and stood between me and Keller.

"Alright," Jane said, "Be on the field in five." She and Louis turned, with the rest of their team in tow, as they went to gather balls and take last sips of water.

"Let's see if you guys got game," Tadd smirked, tapping me on the shoulder as he trotted off to join them.

Hope came over last night, and I explained everything; about being taken off captain, Jenna becoming captain, reuniting with Liv, our team's lack of teamwork, sending the email, and now here, everything, that is, except the conflicting games.

We rejoined with my team and I introduced Hope. I told them about the finger system I had created with her, as a communication form on the field; they all nodded in understanding. Liv, Jenna, Hope and I all stood, looking at each other, confident in our decision to do this, and before we knew it, we were on the field.

The first quarter was rocky, the other team held the score handedly, and they seemed to be dancing circles around us. Hope and I flashed a "2" "1" and she got in a good run, up the sideline with a perfectly placed ball. But when she reached the corner for a turn-in, no one was there to receive it. The other team lead us by three points by half-time. Jane came over and offered to mix the teams, but I turned her down. This was about teamwork, we used to do it, we just needed to forget the past few weeks, and be willing to re-learn.

"Look for passes, call for teammates, put up your numbers. Play based on instinct, not fact. Where do you think they're gonna be, ten seconds into the future? Go there. Where do you think the keeper's gonna toss the ball? Run there. Where do you think the forwards are gonna try and break our line? Be there. Relax, have fun and go play," I said to the team circle. Pep talks were really more for the captains, but no one seemed to mind. We all looked at each other, tapped cleats, and hit the field.

The game restarted in a flurry. A mess of people crowding the ball, too little energy turned to too much. But as the plays went on, the team found its spacing. The defenders formed a triangle, the mids evened out, and the forwards stayed at the line, ready for the pass. Our goalie chucked the ball up the line and our right back, Krista, took it with ease. She looked up and across, lining the ball a five-foot dash to the side of our center-mid. One of the other team's players tried to jump in front of it, but our mid was quicker, snatching the ball, rolling it to the side, and swiftly chipping it over my head.

I ran with it, dodging player after player, determined to bring it all the way. I caught my eye on Liv in the far-right corner, just before the goal. I dashed forward, but the last defender caught me, and I knew I couldn't dribble around this one. I slid across the ground, cutting the ball with me, in a last-ditch effort to grant Liv a viable pass. It was just in from the goal, Tadd ran at it, but Liv went in relentlessly and mimicked my slide, four inches to his left, hitting the goal post and, as luck would have it, bouncing into the net. I ran forward and hugged Liv, hitting cleats, inside, outside, then toe-to-toe. Two points down or not, it felt good to work like that again.

One goal was all the pick-me-up we needed. The game was evenly matched. Our forwards collided with their defense, our mids on their mids, their striker with our sweeper. Our center mid scored off a free kick. Their forwards wove through us and shot another bullet into the bottom corner of our net. Liv rebounded one of their goal kicks and dribbled it twice before stepping back and scoring another one.

We were behind by one, and there were only a few minutes left. I looked to my left to see if my special guest had arrived. Sure enough, she was on the sidelines with a watchful eye. I smiled to myself and shouted "Let's go! Leave it on the field!" to my teammates.

A throw-in kickstarted the last play. A mid-fielder tossed it back to Krista, Krista passed it in to Jenna, and Jenna sent the ball over the half-line to the base of Liv's waiting cleats. She took it up the line, and Hope ran with her. I was still back aways and knew this wasn't my ball. Liv got through their mid-line easily, but the defense surrounded her, stalling, as her opportunity was quickly passing. Tadd crouched, ready for an attempted shot. I watched as Liv hesitated, processing what to do, I saw her look to her sides, trying to decide if she could get around them. I knew she couldn't, but she wasn't one for giving up the ball. To a fault, she'd hold onto it until it was taken from her, determined to prove she could do it. I willed her to play smart, as the seconds felt more like hours. A defender lunged at the ball and she rolled it back, flipping, to guard it from behind. I saw her eyes flash to the side to look for a dribbling opportunity, when she saw Hope, posed and ready to run. She processed, flipped to detract the defenders, and cut the ball to the inside. Hope leapt forward and took the ball in, running past the defenders before they even knew she had the ball. Right as Tadd made his move to run forward, she tapped the ball to the side, and poked it in the goal.

The game was over, and we were tied. I cheered wildly for Hope, running to give her a hug, and high-fiving Liv for a brilliant play. The rest of the team ran forward; we grouped together in excitement. We may not have won in score, but man did we play like winners. The connection was finally back, but our celebration was short-lived. We were cut off by the loud acknowledgement of someone clearing their throat.

"Terry," Liv said.

"What made you come here?" Jenna asked, her confidence faltering.

"I invited her," I said, stepping forward. "She's our coach after all, she should see us play. What'd you think?" I asked, looking her in the eye.

"I think, you all came together to deliberately disrespect me, I have to say I'm disappointed."

"Like I wrote in my email, it was my idea," I admitted. "I don't want to lie, and have fake appointments, and I don't want to just go along with whatever, and

pretend I'm okay with it, I love
soccer, and I love this team, but I
hate our practices, I hate putting
winning above everything else. I can't
speak for them," I gestured to my
team. "But soccer wasn't fun for me
anymore, it's not fun to do drill after
drill, just to get told you're doing
everything wrong. It didn't make me
better, it made me lose my
confidence. But when I came, and
played here, I got it back," I said. "I
just wanted the team to feel that
too."

Liv had been watching the
ground nervously, but looked up at
me when I said that, pride on her
face. Hope had it too. She didn't
know what I said, but she knew I
believed in it, and that was enough.
And when I looked back at Terry, for

the first time, I felt like she looked at me like an equal.

"Do the rest of you feel the same way?" she asked. "Are you glad you came here today instead of practice?" she looked around at the ducking faces, the averted eyes, the slow nods. She sighed. "I am disappointed," she said. "I'm disappointed that I've never seen you girls play like that before. And I realize now that's my own fault." The team looked up in surprise.

"You're not mad?" Jenna asked.

"I'm sad that I drove you to do this. I'm mad you don't play like this for me," she admitted. "But maybe we can change that," she offered the hint of a smile. "We'll scrimmage more at practice, you can take Fridays off to rest before games, and Thursdays, well," she looked thoughtful, "You'll come here."

The team broke into smiles and cheers. "I do expect hard work and dedication," Terry continued, "But, maybe I can trust you to bring that by your own choice."

"You can," I said; Terry looked at me.

"You're still not captain," she clarified, same old Terry.

"I know," I said. "But next time, I deserve to know first." Terry didn't respond directly, but gave me a look that let me know we had an understanding.

"Well I'm off," Terry said, "I'll see you girls Saturday. Keep playing like that, and you'll be ready for the championship on the fourteenth," she said over her shoulder, walking away to her car.

Hope looked at me. I bit my lip and shut my eyes. When I reopened them, my team was dispersing, there were congrats, and pats on the back, everyone getting ready to go, but Hope remained still. She hugged her arm as I saw the beginning of a tear in her eye. She looked at me one more time, and then she was gone.

32

"I still can't believe it," Liv said. "Everything worked perfectly, even better than we thought!" We rounded the corner out of homeroom and made way towards the bike racks. "Terry said that she'd be nicer, *and* that we can keep going to the pick-up games!" she sighed with a smile. "You want to go practice in the park for a while?"

"Not today, I kind of want to take advantage over the whole practice-free Fridays thing," I lied. "I'll meet you at your house to bike to the game tomorrow, yeah?"

"Sounds good," she said, waving me off as she continued on through the neighborhood.

My fake-smile faded as soon as she was out of sight. I unbuckled my helmet and walked my bike over the rest of the sidewalk and up the driveway. I didn't even bother to take my bike into the yard, just left it outside, leaning on the front gate, for the world to see. I went inside the house and shut the door quietly behind me, my mom was at the table working on her computer. She looked up over the rims of her reading glasses, I said hi, but quickly walked back to my room before any further conversation could ensue.

I slid the backpack off my shoulder, and texted Hope for the tenth time, knowing she wouldn't reply. I couldn't make it better, I couldn't lie and say that I didn't realize the conflict. I knew I couldn't do both the moment I looked at those papers. I should have told her right away, but I didn't, I didn't tell her at all. Avoiding the situation didn't solve the problem, it created one.

I let myself fall onto my bed, lying flat, enveloped in the downy comforter, but it didn't bring me comfort at all. Hope had been nothing but understanding in the past about my conflicting feelings, but I didn't even grant her the trust to be understanding about a conflicting schedule. I brought my hands up to my face in frustration, when I remembered they weren't empty. Still clutching my phone, I clicked on the most-called number, and brought it up to my ear.

"Hello, how may I assist you?" a voice clicked on. A station operator.

"Hello, I would like to speak with Lesya Kamenev," I said, trying to hold a strong voice.

"Name."

"Nadia Kamenev."

"One minute please."

The tone clicked off, and I tapped my foot anxiously as I waited. It felt like hours passed before they came back on the phone. "I'm afraid they are out of contact at the moment," the operator said. "Can I leave a message for a future time?"

"Is she okay? I mean, does out of contact mean out of the room, or on the field, or what?" My heart started pounding with fear, and I felt tears beginning to form in the ridges of my eyes.

"I'm afraid I can't give out that information. Can I leave a message?"

My heart sunk and I took a deep breath.

"Please just tell her that her sister called, and that she really needs her."

33

Each day passed slowly, and I still hadn't heard from Hope or Lesya.

Late Friday night, I took off my "LESYA" bracelet, and placed it in a jewelry box she'd given to me before she left. I lay it gently over a photo of the two of us, and touched the top of the box. The same thing I did every time I was worried about her. It had been almost a week since I'd called. It never took her this long to get back to me.

The weekend ended same as it had started off, with me, making mistakes. I had gotten up Saturday morning and rushed out the door, to find my helmet still dangling from the top of the fence, but with nothing below it. My bike had been stolen. I shook my head at my own stupidity, I knew not to leave it unlocked, and beyond that, I knew not to leave it in the front yard at all. I checked my watch, and started at a run for Liv's house.

Once there, we were already behind schedule, and I practically had to sprint alongside her bike in order to get to the game on time. My physical exhaustion, quickly matching the emotional exhaustion I already felt. I took to the field with an overall feeling of weakness.

Still, the games went well, we were definitely in route to the championship. I played hard all weekend, but my heart just wasn't in it. We won twice Saturday in tough matches, and handedly the next day in a 4-0 shutout. Come Sunday, my game was mid-afternoon, keeping me from going to VIP, the last practice of their spring season. Pete told me he'd tell Hope why, but I knew it wouldn't make a difference. It was just me, missing another thing over a team, and coach, I'd spent the last month complaining to her about.

The following week was harder. School, no response, practice, no response, dinner, no response. Everything went slow, and everything felt like a reminder. A reminder I was a bad friend. A reminder I may have lost a friend, who had become one, when I'd lost another. A reminder my sister may be hurt, and there was nothing we could do about it. The damage was done for both situations, all I could do was wait.

My mom was just as worried, but she tried to hide it. She knew I was sad about Hope, and scared about Lesya. She told me that Hope and I would work it out, just give her some time to cool off, then I would apologize, and we could move on. And I knew she believed that. She wasn't concerned about Hope and I, not in the long run; it was about Lesya. She wanted to be the strong one, the backbone for me. Telling me that Lesya would call when she could, that we shouldn't bother her until we hear. But I knew it was just a cover. I heard her calling the station, late at night, trying to use parental rights to get information, but they wouldn't budge. I heard her whisper her worries and prayers. She was just as scared as I was, and that thought terrified me more than anything else.

My mom and Lesya were the two bravest people I'd ever met, compared to them, I felt like a scared little girl, and right now, I didn't have either to lean on.

34

"Nadia, look up!" Liv called.

She shot the ball over my head, but I was too slow in response. The defender reached it before I did, slamming the ball up our line, leaving it to the midfielders to fight over. Before any play could restart, the time ran out, and the game was called. I slumped as I walked off the field, Liv had given me the perfect opportunity, and I had been too distracted to take it. I never missed passes like that. I never gave up so easily.

"Hey, Nadia, wait," Tadd jogged up to me, and touched my right shoulder. I turned to face him with a pale expression.

"Are you okay?" he asked.

"Fine," I said rudely, turning to go.

"You're not fine," he said, touching my shoulder again until I gave in and looked him in the eye. "What's going on?"

I sighed and opened my mouth, but he stopped me before I could get in a word. "And I already know about everything with Hope—" he cut in; I gave him a questioning look. "Liv told me," he explained. "She said it was really bothering you, and I know she's right," he said, "But I also know there's more to it than that, so tell me the truth, are you okay?"

I tried to hold my composure, but seeing the honest concern in his eyes, I broke. I sniffed, and a tear fell down my cheek; I shook my head slowly.

"No," I whispered.

He took a seat in the grass, and patted the ground next to him; I followed suit, brushing a strand of hair behind my ear.

"I feel a lot of guilt about Hope, I feel sad about it," I admitted. "But I also believe that she'll forgive me, and that we'll be okay. I'm upset over that, but I'm mostly just afraid," my head was bobbing as I spoke. "And that has nothing to do with her," I said.

"What is it?"

"My sister," I said.

"From your bracelet?" he asked.

"She's overseas, working as an army nurse," I said. "I tried to call her last Friday, and I haven't heard anything back . . . It just, it never takes this long, and they won't tell us anything." I had a catch in my throat, "What if something's happened to her?" I hugged my knees to my chest, and Tadd allowed me to rest my head on his shoulder.

"You know, when I said I was visiting my brother?" he asked, I nodded in response. "He's in the Air Force, on base out of state," he continued; I looked at him in surprise, immediate empathy washing over me for the lifestyle I was all too familiar with.

"When he first told me he was enlisting, I was terrified. I idolized him growing up, same as you," he looked at me. "But, he always told me that he knew he would be okay, because he had me, and our parents, behind him. We were the reason he was fighting, and no matter what happened, he knew he was doing what was right for him. And if it's right for him, then as his family, it's right for us. I'm sure your sister's the same. Put your trust in her, and keep living your life based on what's right for you," he said, "It's what she would want."

35

Friday afternoon, I evaded Liv's playing request once again. I told her I needed to call Lesya, but refrained from telling her the whole truth, that I wanted to try for the fifth time, even though I knew it would be another blank call. But I called anyway. Another empty operator, giving me the same lack of information. I shuffled around my room, not sure what to do. If I do nothing, I'm going to think about Lesya. If I craft, or bake, I'm going to think about Hope. If I play soccer, I'm going to think about this weekend.

My attempt to stop thinking was cut off by a sound at the door. My mom was out running errands, so, reluctantly, I walked to the foyer. When I went to look out the peephole, I was taken aback by the presence of Hope, patiently waiting on my doorstep. I opened the door to her offering a sad smile, she signed to me that Tadd had told her what was going on. I hugged her, finally letting go of the building tears, she held me for a minute, before releasing and moving to the side, opening my door further to reveal a second person.

"Me too," Liv said. I tilted my head as she came in for a second hug. Together, the three of us went inside, arms linked forward. A triangle, the strongest shape.

As we lay on the couch, there was silence. We would talk for a few minutes, and then there was silence again. Hope rested her head on my shoulder as Liv got up off the couch and began rifling through our DVD drawer.

"That's enough of that," she said. "You need a break. A break from talking, a break from thinking, we need to take you somewhere else," she said dramatically. I waited to see whether or not she was being literal. "You need bravery, you need family, you need a princess, you need. . . Russia," she smirked, holding up a copy of *Anastasia,* my absolute favorite movie growing up. I broke into a smile and nodded, sitting up straighter. Hope recognized the cover and squeezed my hand. Liv popped the disc in and used the remote to skip through commercials right to the movie set up. She clicked subtitles on and pressed play, and through a sea of chandeliers and ballgowns, we were lost to the story of the Romanov's.

"*People always say life is full of choices, no one ever mentions fear*" Anya sang. Watching intimately as she twirled her way through the snow, we didn't even notice my mom walk through the door.

"Nadia, I'm going to start a pasta bake would you like to help?" I heard a faint voice say, then coming closer, "Oh hello girls, would you like to stay for dinner?" I began to lift my head to say something, when my mom came around the corner to see what was on the screen. "Anastasia," she said softly, taking a seat on the chair next to us, "My favorite."

36

The smell of fresh-cut grass filled my nostrils as I treaded across the fields. A ball between my feet, I tapped side-to-side, back-to-front, step-by-step, on my way towards the team. The skies were overcast with grey clouds threatening to drop on us. I burrowed up deeper into the hood of my sweatshirt, breathing heavily into the inner layer to warm it.

After some warm-up runs, I joined the others in a shooting drill. Crosses from each side of the goal-line to the center, girl after girl, charging the passed ball, and claiming it as her own. I was next up on the right side of the goal line; I chipped the ball up and over the head of the temporary defender, slightly to the inside of Liv's feet, just how she likes it. Liv picked the ball up with ease and shot a perfect arch into the top left corner of the goal. I applauded her efforts before jogging upfield to join the shooters line. Two girls ahead of me until my turn arrived, but suddenly, I became stalled in my stance. My stomach churned a huge knot, and out of nowhere, I felt a wave of sickness. *I need electrolytes*, I thought, *I'll go get a drink and I'll be fine.*

As I sat down on the team bench, easing myself into its light padding, I reached for my water, and began snacking on some almonds. I hadn't eaten all day, but even now, I wasn't hungry. As I sat there, I realized it wasn't the dehydration that was making me feel sick to my stomach, it was my nervousness. The idea of another soccer game made me feel sick. How was that going to help Lesya? I shouldn't be out doing things like it's no big deal, not when she might be hurt. I didn't even want to play anymore, not today, not until I heard from her. I thought about saying I was too sick to play, but Tadd's words echoed in my head, *put your trust in her and keep living your life based on what's right for you, it's what she would want.* Hesitantly, and knowing he was right, I got back up and rejoined my team.

Before long, the ref blew the whistle and called up captains, both Liv and Jenna looked at me, but I waved them off, this was their game.

"We're kicking off," Jenna said once they got back. "Staying on this side." The team nodded and got in line as the ref came up to check our equipment. We upturned our cleats, tapped our shin guards, tucked in our shirts, and turned heads to indicate the lack of earrings. He watched each of us carefully, they were always extra strict for championship games.

"Miss," he said, looking at me.

"Yes?"

"I'm gonna need you to take off your bracelet," he pointed at my wrist; I looked down, "HOPE" surrounded by purple and silver beads. My eyes shut gently, I had completely forgotten it was there. I rotated it over my wrist, indicating to the ref that it wasn't an easy twist off.

"You can take a minute to get it off while I check the other team, but I'll need to see its gone before the start of the game," he said, before striding to the other side of the field.

I rolled the beads around their thread, feeling a deep panging sensation in my chest, accompanied by a reluctance to take it off. No matter how upset Hope had been with me, I hadn't felt the need to take it off, and I didn't think she had either. Putting Lesya's in the box was a tradition, a superstition of sorts, but it didn't change anything. It didn't change that she was still with me, that I still heard her voice, and felt the presence of her beliefs. I wondered how she would feel in this situation, and then I realized, the same as me.

"Here, give it to me and I'll put it in that little pocket inside my bag," Liv offered, palm up, holding out her hand. I began to reach to undo the string, when I dropped my hand to my side, letting it dangle.

"I'm okay. Thanks though," I said, looking up at her with a sort of gleeful discovery. "And I'm glad we're kicking off, but you'll be doing it without me."

"What?" Liv questioned, the rest of the team beginning to huddle in towards us. She rolled her eyes and shielded me from them, adding a few yards of distance. "What do you mean do it without you?"

"I can't Liv, I'm sorry," I looked at the ground, hating to disappoint her. "I should be at Hope's game. I

didn't know before but, being here--
I've been lucky enough to play my
whole life, and I'll continue to play
my whole life, but Hope . . . she
hasn't been that lucky. This may be a
championship game for us, and hers
may be 'just a game', but I guarantee
you, that game means more to her,
than this one does to me."

"Then go," Liv smiled, without
pause, ducking her head to look me
in the eye.

"Really?" I asked in surprise.
"What about them? They won't get
it," I gestured at the team, still
watching, waiting to hear what was
going on.

"I'll deal with them," Liv said,
"And Terry," she winked. "And who
cares? They don't have to get it. I

know how much your friendship with Hope means to you, so go, it's okay," she smiled and I hugged her. "And take my bike," she said, putting me at arm's length, "You'll get there a lot faster."

"Thank you, Liv."

"Thank me later, go!" she said, shooing me away, I laughed and ran off towards the bikes. Terry called after me to see where I was going, but I just kept running, I had to get there.

I undid Liv's bike in a flurry, pedaling faster than I ever had before, looking down at my watch every few seconds for motivation. And before I knew it, I was there. I dropped the bike against a tree and dashed off, only to come back a few seconds later and lock it, I probably shouldn't get Liv's bike stolen too. The game had already started and Hope was on the field. I glanced around the sidelines for familiar faces, jogging up the line.

"What'd I miss?" I asked innocently.

"Just started a few minutes ago but—Nadia?" Tadd turned to find me in shock, "You came! How'd your team do?" he asked.

"I think they'll do really well," I said.

"So, you haven't played yet today?" he asked.

"No," I said, "And I'm not going to." He gave me a questioning look and I crossed my arms, "It's called a team for a reason," I said. "A player can change a play, but not a game. If they can do it with me, they can do it without me," I shrugged, "Besides, as good as it feels to win; it feels a whole lot better when the person winning isn't you, but someone you care about."

"Right for you?" he asked.

"Right for her," I said; he smiled. "And by the way, next time someone tells you all about their family drama, you might not want to go expose it to everyone they know."

"I didn't, I didn't mean to—"

"Relax," I said, "And thank you."

"You're welcome," he said. "Now, let's make sure someone sees you," he pushed me forward, and I fell on my hands, exposed at the front of the group line. Hope looked up and immediately her expression changed, she waved excitedly, rushing back into the game with even greater intensity.

"Hey, Nadia, glad you could make it," Pete said, not noticing my arrival until after I hit I grass.

"Glad to be here," I said, glaring up at Tadd and brushing off my shorts.

The air was sticky hot, and there were only a few minutes left in the game. I held my hands together and watched anxiously. The other team was up 2-1, and everyone was exhausted. Hope held her hands on her hips, sucking in boughs of air, as the midfielders fought over the ball a few meters to her right. Their time was running out.

I caught her eye and touched my bracelet, subtly holding up four fingers; she nodded and threw herself in the dog pile. It was a fluster of cleats and legs, with a ball playing ping-pong back and forth between the two. It appeared an endless fight, until one leg reached in for the ball, put their heel in front of it, and hit it backwards like a bullet. Hope flipped around and ran with it, all before the other players even recognized what had happened.

She moved forward faster than I'd ever seen, and charged the goal. She flew through the defenders, matching the keeper head-to-head. They dove at her feet, and without hesitation, she rolled the ball backwards, up her calf, and flipped it over her head, landing on the other side of the goalie, and perfectly placed for her to flick it past the line.

She did the rainbow in a real game. I couldn't believe it, and she couldn't either, she beamed, almost in state of shock that it had worked. I jumped up and cheered, as the ref blew the final whistle. I wanted to run out there, but didn't. I knew that they needed to meet the opposing team and thank the refs, but Hope didn't, she bounded towards me and met me for a hug. She was radiating with joy, and my heart was touched with pride. I signed to her what a great job she did, and she shuffled nervously, looking up at me.

"Thank, you, Nadia," Hope pronounced slowly. My words caught in my throat, my heart felt full and I forgot everything else. Tears gathered in my eyes, not believing what I heard. How did she do it? Who had taught her? How long had she been practicing? She smiled at my reaction, taking a deep breath as though relieved by my happiness. Then, she glanced up and a look of shock graced her expression.

"Lesya?" she spoke with less certainty. My heart immediately sank, I shook my head.

"No, I haven't heard," I signed along with my words.

"Um, I don't think that's what she's asking," Tadd stated, walking up and pointing behind me. I whipped around and my voice cracked like a million shards.

"Lesya!" I cried.

Heart pounding, I bolted to where my sister leaned against a tree just before the lot. She dark hair had been cut, shorter than I'd last seen it. Her brown eyes as warm and inviting as ever. I rushed into her arms, melting like butter and breaking into streams of tears. But, I pulled back quickly when I saw her wince, for the first time, noticing her right arm tucked high in a sling.

"What happened! How are you? How long are you home? What did mom tell you? How'd you even find me?" I asked.

"Whoa, slow down," she said, splaying her hands. "I went by home first, mom told me you'd be here," she expressed.

"How? I didn't tell her, that wasn't even the plan!" I gasped in amazement. Still in disbelief she was even in front of me.

"It may not have been where you were going this morning, but she knew this is where you'd end up," she whispered.

"I just can't believe you're here," I hugged her again; she held me tight.

"I told you I'd be okay," she said.

"Thank you," I said.

"For what? Being okay?" she laughed.

"Everything," I said. "I couldn't have done it without you, any of it."

"What do you mean, I wasn't here," she said. "I didn't even know about the conflicting games, this was all you."

"You don't have to be here," I said, realizing it as I said it. "You've given me such a great example of what love, and life, is really about. You could be anywhere in the world, and you would still lead me, just in the way you live. So, thank you."

She tilted her head with a smile and the promise of tears, tucking a strand of hair behind my ear. But before she could respond, Hope and Tadd rushed up behind us. I laughed at their eagerness and gave introductions all around, but, before I could even finish that, right on cue, Liv ran up to us. Her dad honking from the seat of his car as he drove away.

"We won!" she cried, holding out of her medal proudly, and clutching a second one for me. "Can you believe it?" I nudged my head to the side, and her eyes followed my movement. "Lesya!" she screamed, wrapping her in a hug. "You're back! And you're okay! This is amazing!"

"Okay-ish," I pointed out, looking at her swollen shoulder. "Now explain," I said, like a parent to a child who'd missed curfew.

"Trust me, I'll tell you everything," she promised. "But let's get home, I'm starving, and mom's making—" she stopped short, "Wait a minute, Liv, isn't that your bike?" She pointed at the tree adjacent to us, then turned to me: "Where's yours?"

"Uh, long story," I laughed. "But don't worry," I hugged her good arm, "What of mine I lose, I'll get back. You're living proof of that."